A native of Lowell, Massachusetts, James Grand has lived mostly in New York City and Southern California. Winning a national creative writing competition while in law school encouraged him to consider an idea for a novel – a form of writing far from the legal briefs and formalities of his profession. It was during his first visit to Buenos Aires that he was inspired to tell the story of "Then Came Morning." James and his husband, Stephen, now enjoy life in Rancho Mirage, California.

Then Came Morning

James Grand

Then Came Morning

Vanguard Press

VANGUARD PAPERBACK

© Copyright 2024
James Grand

The right of James Grand to be identified as author of
this work has been asserted by him in accordance with the
Copyright, Designs and Patents Act 1988.

All Rights Reserved

No reproduction, copy or transmission of this publication
may be made without written permission.
No paragraph of this publication may be reproduced,
copied or transmitted save with the written permission of the publisher, or in
accordance with the provisions
of the Copyright Act 1956 (as amended).

Any person who commits any unauthorised act in relation to this publication
may be liable to criminal prosecution and civil claims for damages.

A CIP catalogue record for this title is available from the British Library.

ISBN 978-1-83794-378-4

This is a work of fiction. Names, characters, businesses, places, events and
incidents are either the products of the author's imagination or used in a
fictitious manner. Any resemblance to actual persons, living or dead, or actual
events is purely coincidental.

Vanguard Press is an imprint of
Pegasus Elliot Mackenzie Publishers Ltd.
www.pegasuspublishers.com

First Published in 2024

Vanguard Press
Sheraton House Castle Park
Cambridge England

Printed & Bound in Great Britain

Dedication

To Stephen, my husband and inspiration

Prologue

It had rained during the night. The yellowish light of the streetlamps reflected off the wet flagstones, off the limestone façade of the Ministerio de Economía, and off the marble stairs of the Catedral Metropolitana. Despite the weather, hundreds of Perón loyalists had gathered in the Plaza de Mayo before daybreak in a show of support. Taking advantage of the clouds still hovering over Buenos Aires, the Navy's fixed-wing raptors broke formation, banked sharply and suddenly burst into sight. Every window shuttered in anticipation. On their second pass, they fired on the *Casa Rosada*, the presidential residence, and strafed the surrounding ministry buildings, killing more than three hundred of the assembled Peronistas. The year was 1955. The unfolding coup sent Juan Perón into exile in Spain and set the stage for the barbaric events that unfolded twenty-one years later.

Perón returned from exile in 1973 and found himself ruling over an increasingly violent split in the Peronist movement. Cities throughout Argentina increasingly were plagued by shootings, daily bombings, kidnappings and random violence. Buenos Aires, in particular, was torn by terror from both the extreme right and the far left. Anyone with money hired bodyguards and paid both sides for protection.

By the middle of the 1970s, the country was exhausted and wanted change. In a nonviolent coup in March 1976, General Santiago Rafael Videla became *de facto* president. Immediately after taking office, Videla and three other generals comprising a four-person junta stepped onto the Casa Rosada's famous balcony and introduced sweeping measures to combat 'subversion'. They came up with a plan called the Process for National Reorganization or, simply, the Process—a mundane and benign name for the savagery that followed.

Videla effectively declared war against his own countrymen: anyone whose activities, even thoughts, were deemed subversive. Toward the end of the speech and to thunderous applause, he pounded the railing with his left fist to emphasize how harshly the military regime would deal with 'subversives'.

Drawing on the generals' considerable oratory skills, the Process—*El Proceso*—was sold to Argentinians with language that duped their capacity to reason and lent respectability to a lie. Videla and his generals deliberately exaggerated the 'terrorist' threat to give themselves military authority that went well beyond even the considerable emergency powers the military acquired just one year before to prosecute what it then called its 'war against subversion'. Braced with immunity and fresh new powers bordering on absolute, they gradually convinced an exhausted nation that its freedoms had to be temporarily sacrificed in the name of 'security'. Argentinians had no way of knowing their acquiescence to such a bargain freed the military to ignore the basic human rights that were laid down in the constitutions of every civilized nation on Earth, including Argentina.

All sectors of Argentinian society fell into the military's wide net. It didn't matter whether you actually were involved with subversive groups; it was enough to belong to a segment of society that was suspected of having socialist leanings. Intellectuals, social workers, union members, writers, journalists and their like were presumed to have leftist tendencies. Students suffered disproportionately. The universities were purged within months of the coup, resulting in widespread arrests among young pacifists, student leaders, and those who merely were unfortunate enough to be listed in the wrong person's address book.

The generals' tactics became more than a means to an end. Violence came to be viewed as a restorative force—a bloodletting that was necessary to restore civility. Those who were targeted by the regime were kidnapped by uniformed security forces operating in secret under the cover of night. Come morning; distraught family members would be shuffled between their local police precincts and the military security forces. Either or both would claim to have no knowledge of any police action taking place in the vicinity of the missing person's abduction. There would be no record of the missing person being held in official custody. Morning, then, became an hour when amnesia was convenient, and hope became an eternal, private dusk.

Of course, the captives were in custody, inevitably in one of the three hundred or so secret detention centers across Argentina, where they were subjected to prolonged and horrific torture. Electric prods, sexual abuse and waterboarding were common. Physical torture was often accompanied by psychological torture. Captives would be hooded for weeks and months, lined up for mock executions or forced to watch their spouses and children being raped and tortured; babies were harvested from pregnant women, frequently by forced, late-night Caesarian sections. The newborns were confiscated by their captors—usually to be sold or given to military couples who were having difficulty conceiving. Bodies occasionally reappeared in the street, deliberately made to appear as if they had been killed in a shoot-out with the police. The remains of thousands are believed to have been encased in the freshly poured cement walls of the new subway then under construction in Buenos Aires. Some were transported to remote locations, doused with gasoline and burned, then buried in mass graves other captives had been forced to dig. Others were drugged and put on 'death flights'. These were flights flown over the Atlantic Ocean in the darkest hours. The sedated captives were thrown into the sea to drown—so-called 'fish food'. The generals assumed that without bodies, there would be no evidence of their horrific crimes. People just 'disappeared'.

Part One

Coming of Age
In the Time of the Generals

Buenos Aires, 1977

1977 is remembered by most Argentinians as the time of the generals. But to kids like me, schoolboys waiting in our yet inchoate world for the future to reveal itself, life goes on pretty much as usual. The only really noticeable change in our daily routine is the obligatory school assemblies at which we listen to broadcast speeches and proclamations from General Videla himself or one of the other three military members of the junta. They infuse their rhetoric with double-talk about democracy and slather it with the new vocabulary—words and phrases like terrorists, criminals, subversives and enemies of freedom. At the end of each convocation, we dutifully rise, face the nation's celeste and white standard and, eyes focused on the gold sunburst at its center, listen as the gravelly strains of our national anthem issue from the loudspeakers on each side of the stage, our freshly-minted baritone voices joining in each time the band repeats the only lyric we know by heart: *El Gran Pueblo Argentino, Salud!*

Very little is said at school about the events taking place around us. Teachers won't answer questions about the Process, usually saying it is a difficult topic that we have not progressed far enough in our studies to understand. When pressed hard, they say a small group of criminals is planting bombs in such-and-such places, seeking to impose their ideas on society, and the military is trying to restore order.

Not much more is said at home. "There is nothing to fear," says my mother. "As long as we are not involved in anything, they will leave us alone."

But I am afraid. Without meaning to, my mother subtly conveys the presence and nearness of danger.

"Don't talk to anyone more than absolutely necessary, and be careful what you say," she warns. "Don't draw attention to yourself or get involved in crowds of people. If you see something unusual, look away. It's better not to get involved." Everyone else did the same during those times: ignore what was happening in our city as though it had nothing to do with us.

*

There is no official curfew, but everyone knows the streets must empty well before nightfall. A few cafes and bars stay open, but their customers are mostly people who need refuge until the first coppery rays of sunlight make it safe to venture out again. Military vehicles are the only traffic, convoys of cars and trucks that have been appropriated by the junta and repainted dark green. Their occupant's faces, usually covered with black masks, defiantly brandish long weapons in plain view, creating an unsettling combination of anonymity and ostentation that heightens the terrorizing effect.

"Look at them," said Sr. Rouquié as a convoy passed outside the window. "A bunch of thugs. If they have legal orders, they wouldn't be ashamed of showing their faces."

As Rouquié is speaking, more convoys of canopied green trucks meander by, their true mission and destination a mystery. Sometimes, they are accompanied by the dull green Ford Falcons, which is a standard issue of the Navy's secret police. No one can express their fear very precisely, but like the pale green raptor from which it gets its name, Falcons are dreaded beasts, meat eaters that hunt for prey under the cover of darkness, usually swooping down at lightning speed. A Falcon has only to stop outside a café, and its patrons cower in fear until it moves on. Everyone knows people who have been taken away.

*

I live with my mother in a rented third-floor apartment on the fringe of what is now called Microcentro, the city's financial and commercial center. The building, stout and unremarkable, faces a once pretty but now squalid square at the intersection of Calle Esmeralda and Tucumán, which is lined with cafes and garishly neon-lit *farmacias*. Our building's begrimed stone façade is an unworthy postscript to the stately hotel it had been in better times when the neighborhood had its own name, San Nicolás, and a reputation as the capital's entertainment center.

My mother is a solitary woman, although not given to self-pity or depression. Her life is raising me; she doesn't seem to care for another living person. Her mother died young, and as befitted her upbringing as the only child of a bookseller, she experiences the world through fictional characters, not heroines and heiresses, but ingénues and women whose lives had not turned out quite as they expected.

Our apartment is cheerless but not drab. That is if you overlooked the limp curtains and faded vines and roses climbing the yellowing wallpaper. The living room has two floor-to-ceiling windows that open onto little balconies with rusted, vase-shaped balustrades. It is filled with odd 'finds' that once belonged to others. There is a lacquered desk with a creaky wooden chair, two unsightly stuffed chairs, one with a cigarette burn in the floral upholstery, a gold-trimmed Luis XIV buffet, sagging bookshelves and a dull Persian carpet with threadbare patches here and there.

My room is small and crammed with teen stuff. Like most Argentinian boys, I am crazy about soccer and am already looking forward to the World Cup, which will be held in Argentina next year. My walls are covered with magazine clippings and team jerseys. Pictures of my favorite players, some of which are autographed, are taped to the mirror frame: Ubaldo Fillol in the goal, Osvaldo Ardiles and, of course, Mario Kempes—*El Matador*. The top of my bureau is cluttered with various sundries, a framed photograph of my late father, an eight-track cassette player, a rare piece of mail and a cigar box full of coins. Clothes are strewn on the floor amidst soccer balls and well-worn sneakers. My private refuge is a single twin bed where I masturbate to my fantasies most evenings as cars slowly wind their way through an atonal symphony of noisy streets, distant sirens, horns, sputtering engines and grinding gears.

*

If someone had said my life in that apartment was dull, I wouldn't have understood. Because it is what I know, so to my way of thinking, it is normal. It never occurred to me that it may have seemed dull to my mother, although I sense her life has not turned out as she once dreamed, that things have been disappointing for her.

Every year, on the anniversary of my father's death, my mother keeps me out of school. We get up early and go down to the cemetery and put a vase of fresh flowers outside my father's crypt, then have lunch in a proper restaurant. I have never met my father's parents and learned pretty much everything I know about them on those annual June days. They were from Rosario. My father was their favorite son, and when he was a teenager, his father sent him away to a prestigious military school. That isn't much to know, and it has not occurred to me to ask to know more.

My father apparently fit squarely into the military mold of being loyal, disciplined and imperious. Upon graduation, he was assigned to the military barracks in Buenos Aires. There, he met and courted my mother. She was then just twenty-one and a recent graduate in literature from the University of Buenos Aires.

The military discourages fraternization with civilians. Officers generally marry the daughters of local dignitaries or into other military families. Because of this tradition, when my father announced his engagement to my mother, my grandfather apparently objected, fearing his son's military career would be damaged. Over his objections, my father convinced his superior officer to marry him in a military chapel. The reading at their wedding was chosen by my mother from her favorite Pablo Neruda poem, *In My Sky at Twilight,* and read by one of my father's comrades: *You are mine, mine, a woman with sweet lips, and in your life, my infinite dreams live.*

My father's parents treated my mother in a way that instilled in her a dismissive loathing for the military that lasts until this day. She is disdainful of the arrogance of military power and silently chafes when military motorcades careen through traffic or officers walk straight to the head of a line, oblivious to the civilians patiently waiting their turn. It has never been spoken in so many words, but nevertheless, it is clear she does not want me to follow in my father's footsteps. She views soldiers as brutes and the military as the career of last resort for slow and erring sons. "Soldiers are trained to obey and kill," she would say, "not to think."

By all accounts, my mother loved my father, but not the programmed regime he was trained to live by. She liked books, scholarship, and permanence; the climate in the home she was born and raised in was tolerant and urbane. When she became pregnant with me, she beseeched my father to leave the military. She pleaded that she did not want me to grow up dutifully moving every two years to a new post. While that was true, her more deeply held reason was different. She wanted me to be intellectual, to attend university—to learn and question and make informed decisions. The matter, however, would be moot. My father died unexpectedly two months before I was born.

Though she had been a devoted wife, soon after my birth, my mother and my father's parents began to quarrel. She believed my father had some money in a trust fund and demanded that they provide for me. In the final meeting she had with them, my stern-faced grandfather insisted my mother was still young and capable of remarrying and, in the meantime, she would have to make do with my father's military pension. Eventually, she discovered that my father had some modest investments with which she opened a separate bank account to be used solely for my university tuition. She never touched this money, which she always referred to as 'your father's', except in an emergency, like the time I broke my wrist when I was sixteen years old.

We got by mainly by adjusting our needs to fit our means. We moved into our current apartment, and she took a job working weekdays in a small hotel conveniently located two blocks from the apartment. Her income was meager, but it covered the rising costs of supporting me—a growing boy.

The hotel was on the fringe of shabby but still a bit genteel and respectable. My mother, characteristically efficient, could manage the reception desk, answer the telephone and keep the records. She collected the foreign newspapers and magazines the guests occasionally left behind and read them from front to back. They were her sustenance—a book lover's furtive line to uncensored thoughts and ideas and the larger world she had dreamed to know. She paid no attention to the state television news or the local newspapers. She did not believe anything they said.

Ever since my mother started working at the hotel, I have been going there right after school and doing my homework in a small room behind the reception desk. When my mother's shift is over, we usually dine on leftovers in the brightly lit, white-tiled kitchen and then walk home together. One night, we turned the corner onto our street just as two of the notorious Falcons and a Jeep entered, going slowly in the wrong direction. My mother immediately turned me away. "Don't look at anything; just look down." In single file, the vehicles threaded their way down the street, gravel popping under their tires. Finally, the slow sweep of headlights passed. We could look up.

*

Throughout my childhood, we lived a solitary life in the apartment: my mother and me, a single mother and a boy on the path to becoming a man. I know from old photographs that she was once an attractive young woman, but she always seemed old to me. Perhaps it was because, despite always being neatly dressed, her clothes were dowdy, and her straight hair was graying in silvery streaks. Oddly, she took no pains against it. This would have been an endearing quality if it was traceable to a lack of narcissism. But in my mother's case, it was a sign that she was defeated and worn down. She was only thirty-eight, but to me, she looked and seemed much older.

My mother believed in the power of knowledge, often pointing to the fact that there seemed to be a bookstore on every block in Buenos Aires as visible proof that Argentina was a civilized and exceptionally literate society. When she wasn't working at the hotel or preparing a meal, she would take to 'her' chair in the living room and pick up one of the increasingly scarce books that she was always reading or re-reading. When I had nothing else to do—which was too much of the time—I found myself mimicking the same behavior. Books eased my friendlessness and became my window beyond the block on which I lived and the mysteries of Buenos Aries. Through them, I learned that my life was different than other boys. Just how different I was curious to find out.

Occasionally, I would find a picture of my father stuck between the pages of a forgotten book. My favorite is the one with my mother, taken at their wedding. He is wearing his military dress uniform and looking sharp, crisp and confident. His skin is taught across the prominent features of his face, his cap resting on his brow—almost too large for his narrow head. I doubt he would look like that today. Like my mother, he would probably be heavier and, perhaps, a bit less sure of himself.

Until about four years ago, when I was about thirteen and a half, I didn't think I missed having a father. But then I started thinking more about it, wondering what he would be like and what kind of relationship we would have. For some reason, I imagined he would be distant, perhaps captive inside. I couldn't think of much he would do for me that my mother couldn't. But as I got older, I started thinking differently.

I remember one time when I really could have used him. I think it was just after my fifteenth birthday, which my mother and I celebrated alone, naturally. I noticed a pimple at the base of my penis. Over the next two days, it became bright pink and rose into an angry sore. I was convinced this was payback for my secret pleasures. On the third night, I called into the living room and asked my mother to come into my room. As she crossed the threshold, she immediately sensed something was wrong and rushed to the side of my bed. As she always had in these situations since I was a child, she automatically put her hand on my forehead to see if I was feverish.

Turning my head into the pillow, I said I have a problem and then added shyly, "Down there."

Resigned to what would have to be done now, I pushed down my pajama bottoms. I was certain she couldn't help but see that I had done this to myself and avoided her eyes. After what seemed forever, she assured me that it was just an ingrown hair. For a moment, I lay still, aware that she was looking down at me, fearing that she was thinking I was a degenerate.

When I got home the next day, my mother was stationed in her usual chair in the sitting room; she seemed troubled and patted the sofa next to her, a signal for me to sit down. I was certain she was going to say something about me masturbating. In carefully measured words, she asked if I would like to talk with a man about the changes taking place in my body. She explained that she was unaware I had grown up so much, and it was time I talked with someone who could tell me things about life that a father normally explained to his sons. That was perhaps the most intimate moment I had ever spent with her. Yet, I demurred. She was silent. But what came next surprised me: she wanted me to get out more and find some friends.

"What interests you?" she asked. "We haven't talked much about it, but surely you must have interests."

But I didn't; at least, I couldn't think of any at that moment.

"Do you have friends at school?" she asked.

"Yes, of course," I lied.

Sensing that, she suggested that maybe I needed to be involved in something other than soccer, where I would meet new people.

"Perhaps you could get involved in a reading program at the library or do odd jobs at the hotel, just something to be around other boys."

I nodded.

"Well, we'll think of something," she added. She came over to where I was sitting, bent down and kissed me on the forehead. "You're a good boy, Paul."

Her tender kiss made me feel uncomfortable.

"Maybe I will get involved with the student center at my school," I said, almost as an afterthought.

She quickly and firmly ruled out the idea. "It's better to stay away from the student center. I don't want you on any lists."

I didn't understand why she was telling me this, but, as usual, she said she knew what was best for me. I later learned that the student centers were seen as a breeding ground for activism, and the military authorities were tracking their members.

*

When my mother and I talked about me getting out more and what interested me, there was one thing I wanted to mention, but sensing that she would not approve, I didn't. I had been going to a nearby gym after school off and on and was getting to know a few of the trainers there. One of them, a nineteen-year old physical therapy student named Agustin, was teaching me how to use the weights in his spare time. I became interested in resistance training and read everything about it that I could get my hands on. I was determined to look like the men in the exercise magazines and even started thinking that maybe one day I might follow Agustin into the study of physical therapy.

After going there several times, I told my mother about my plan. I wanted to join this gym. After a day or so of coaxing, she gave me permission and even agreed to let me use some of my father's money to pay for it. On the condition that I would be home at least thirty minutes before dark, I started working out three nights a week, often until the gym closed at dusk.

The gym occupied the top floors of a four-story limestone building on Calle Paraguay, one of many deteriorating art nouveau mansions in the area. Its once gleaming limestone was now begrimed with glued posters, stencils, soot and graffiti. At the top of four flights of creaking stairs there was a small café you passed through to get to the locker room.

When Agustin was not training a client, he worked behind the bar, checking membership cards, making coffee drinks, adjusting the music and handing out thin, frayed white towels. The weights and exercise machines were on the mezzanine, interspersed lines of clunky machines on which people biked, ran and rowed. There was a large, heated swimming pool above, on the solarium level, under a rusty, hangar-shaped retractable roof. Its humid, chlorine-saturated air, combined with the rest of the gym's smell of sweat, gives the entire place a wooly, soothing feel. According to the old stenciling that was peeling from the walls leading to the shower room, there used to be a Turkish bath. As far as anyone knew, however, its doors had been locked for years.

I looked forward every day to climbing the gym's creaky old stairs and quickly came to feel at home there.

Part of the reason was Agustin. Surprisingly, we developed an easy friendship.

Agustin was someone that people noticed and about whom they asked—who's that? He had Nordic, angular features and was striking and handsome. There was no denying his resemblance to the young warriors imagined by ancient Greek artisans. His light skin, dark blonde curls and attentive green eyes—rarities in Argentina—gave him a look that can only be described as extraordinary. It was hard to isolate the source of his appeal. He just had 'it', that effortless thing naturally popular people have without realizing it.

After I had been going to the gym steadily for about a month, I began to notice my body was changing. My shoulders seemed to be getting broader. My mother noticed it, too and warned me not to get carried away. "You don't want to hurt yourself," she kept saying. She also noticed I seemed happier and interpreted this as a sign that I was making friends.

There was another change, noticeable only to me, for which I didn't have a name at the time. I was becoming infatuated with Agustin, thinking about him constantly. When I got home from the gym, I would go right to my bedroom and try to emulate his gestures in front of my mirror. For the first time, I saw someone I liked and wanted to be—tall, filling out, almost handsome. Confusing yet exhilarating thoughts of Agustin started coming to me in the nighttime.

*

In Buenos Aires, the days get hot in December, the beginning of the austral summer. Around Christmas, it's almost eleven o'clock before the intensely hot sun finally sets. More and more lately, I caught myself in the throes of tedium, perhaps not unrelated to my somewhat growing desire to be among other people—thanks to my experience with Agustin. My room was stifling. It became impossible to concentrate. Taking care to return before dark, on the nights I did not go to the gym, I started venturing out for walks in the twilight, a lone figure seeking a break from the heat and isolation that were bearing down on me.

It had been a long time since I had ventured out at dusk. At first, I was spooked by the fading, eerie light. For a while, the furthest I traveled was Avenida Corrientes, just three blocks from the apartment. Corrientes was once the center of Buenos Aires' entertainment district. It was always crowded and well-lit, and I enjoyed looking at the movie posters in the windows of the two theatres that were still operating.

One particularly hot evening when the temperature had set a record, I stopped at a small restaurant on the corner of Rodriguez Peña, just a few blocks from home. I seated myself at a table in the window—a seventeen-year-old kid, obviously alone, possibly lost. The lights were off as a gesture to the heat. The windows were open wide, but the air inside smelled of frying meat and was greasy, close and still. The lone fan was aimed at the cook. Everyone was fanning themselves and complaining about the humidity.

I ordered a cheeseburger from the sticky plastic menu, *hamburguesa con queso*, which was cheap but sufficient. From across the room, a girl, a young woman actually, seemed to be staring at me. I figured her to be nineteen, maybe twenty. She was shorter than me and somewhat pretty. If I wasn't so shy, I may have been 'interested' in her. But instead, I looked away and concentrated on the humming fan and the sounds and smells of the restaurant.

Sports news was playing on a black-and-white television hanging over the counter. The reception was poor, and the sound was low, but I could hear the announcer saying something about the World Cup. A note of excitement or anticipation stirred in me as I gazed at the blinking screen. I got up and moved closer to the set, shyly avoiding eye contact with the girl who, I sensed, was still looking at me. I reached the counter in time to hear Coach Menotti discussing *la nuestra*.

*

When I returned to my table, the girl looked my way again, this time passing me a shy glance. Her meal was on the table in front of her, but she wasn't eating. Her attention seemed to be focused on me alone. It was strangely uncomfortable. When I finally rose to leave, it didn't surprise me that she did the same.

I walked slowly, aimlessly, toward Avenida Callao, considering my options. I was curious to know where this awkward dance was leading and vaguely aroused. Deciding it might make sense to let her catch up, I stopped, pretending to look in a shoe store window. She approached slowly, passed silently, and then turned and looked back: two teen strangers, each feigning indifference.

She spoke first. Her name was Maya. I told her mine was Eduardo. I don't know why I didn't give her my real name. I just didn't. We stood in front of the window making cautious small talk, each nervously shifting weight from leg to leg. After a while, the conversation was easy, and we walked together. I was surprised and nervous when she told me we had arrived at the door to her apartment on Calle Ecuador. As she fished through her purse for the key, I asked myself one last time if I was going to go through with what I expected might happen.

Maya's apartment was small and curiously furnished; 'student housing', she called it. She was studying to become a nurse. Medical books were open on the kitchen table, a white uniform hung on a door that led to the bathroom. The bare living room walls were covered with moisture-stained wallpaper, the pattern barely visible.

I finally got a closer look at her. I figured she was Spanish or Italian—light brown skin, sharp features, and large coffee-colored eyes. I was getting aroused and asked timidly if we should sit down. When she joined me on the couch my mind was reeling. I wondered if she could tell I had never been with a girl. Instead of sitting next to me, she suggested we go into the bedroom.

I guess I hesitated.

"Are you coming?" she asked.

As soon as we fell backward onto her bed, I moved my hand into the warmth between her legs. As I pushed down her jeans, she tugged at mine. But for some inexplicable reason, when she finally fished out my penis, it wasn't stiff.

"Am I doing something wrong?" she asked.

"No, it's not that."

"Don't you like me?" she asked. A moment's pause and then the question I most dreaded. "Are you like… a *maricón*?"

"No," I chirped. "It's definitely not that." But that's not what I was thinking. I was wondering what this said about me.

Maya was speaking now in a hushed tone, choosing her words and saying them carefully as though saying the wrong thing now might hurt or, worse, damage me. She took my hand and put it up to her cheek.

"Relax," she said. "You're nervous."

Timidly, I said I should zip up my pants. She schussed me and pushed them down further to my knees and then, taking my cock and balls in her hands, started squeezing, gently at first and then harder. Her caresses felt good, but fear and anxiety seized me when it was apparent that I was still not erect. I pushed her hands away and sat up, motionless. I couldn't think of anything to say; suddenly, everything seemed wrong. I felt self-conscious sitting there like that. But even though I wanted to, I couldn't have moved. We sat for minutes in strained silencer.

"What happened tonight... or didn't happen—"

Maya interrupted before I could finish my thought. "Don't think any more about it."

"Well, I really wanted it to happen," I said. "I don't know why I couldn't."

*

Without either of us realizing it, the evening was rapidly approaching night. The remains of the day had been imperceptibly fading by those long minutes. The evening sky of the hour before had become an inky blue-black canopy stained by the mercury vapor lights of the inner city.

"It's too dark for you to be on the streets. It's too late and dangerous for you to go home."

It was about twelve blocks to my apartment, ten minutes if I walked briskly. It was after curfew, but it wasn't really too late, I thought. *There might still be people out on Avenida Corrientes, and if there weren't, I would stick to the back streets where it was less likely there would be patrols.*

But Maya persisted and wanted me to sleep on her couch. "Everything's cool," she said.

I was worried about my mother. I knew she would think something had happened to me and be frantic. Also,

I really wanted to be alone. I needed to be in my own bedroom where I could think. Thinking it might be getting more dangerous as it grew darker, I decided it would be better if I left right then before it got any later.

As soon as I stepped outside Maya's door, I could see Corrientes to my right. As I hoped, there were still some cars and an occasional person walking purposefully. Before taking my first step, I listened to the night. At my feet, a few pigeons warbled softly and milled around, their claws scratching the tiles. Otherwise, the quiet was so deep I thought I could hear my pulse. I heard a window close somewhere on the block and a dog barking in the distance. I walked straight for the lights of Corrientes, taking care to make no noise and to stay in the shadows. I was alone when I reached the avenue and turned left onto the wide sidewalk. There was no one else in sight. I walked a half block along Corrientes and stepped into the vestibule of a *Banelco* to reassess my situation. If a car approached, I could duck back and be out of sight. Within minutes, three military cars passed. I watched as they sped through the orange patches of streetlight. It sounded like they turned on a street a few blocks away. Moments later, screeching brakes broke the total, black silence.

I did not expect to see a military patrol this early. I knew in some parts of me that this was risky, probably a mistake. But I kept thinking, what else can I do? I was worried about my mother. I really needed to get away from Maya, at least for now. The papers were saying only political activists and terrorists were the military's prime suspects, not a boy like me. I didn't know whether I believed that, but still, it was worrying.

I froze up every time another car approached. There was no way of knowing for sure if they were military vehicles until they were upon me, so I assumed they might be. Too many minutes had ticked off, and I felt my only option was to return to Maya's. But, by now, I was afraid to move, fearing more military vehicles would be following the ones that had just passed.

It was no more than twenty meters back to the corner. I debated whether it would be best to make a run for it as if caught in a sudden rainstorm or just walk normally. I heard my mother's voice telling me to avoid acting suspiciously. It hurt terribly to think of her; she would be in total panic. After cautiously poking my head out just far enough to look up and down Corrientes and seeing that no one else was about, I casually stepped into the open and, with my head down and forward and hands in both pockets, walked normally. The short walk seemed to take forever. As if in a dream, my feet seemed stuck. What relief I felt when I was finally back under the cover of darkness.

*

Not more than twenty minutes had passed, but Maya's lights were out. Her windows were already shuttered. I didn't know what to do, and for a moment, I reconsidered whether I could make it home along the back streets. Thinking better of it, I called out Maya's name softly at first and then, gradually abandoning caution, louder. No lights came on, but I was sure people were watching me from behind shutters that had been cracked open just the slightest bit. When Maya finally opened the front door, I was really scared; I just wanted to be safe until the sun came up.

"Are you all right?" she asked, looking me over and hurriedly pulling me in from the street and out of sight.

"Yes, yes."

"I heard some cars and feared they had stopped for you."

"They stopped a few blocks away. Everything is okay. No one saw me." My heart was pounding.

"Are you sure?" she asked. "They might—"

"Yes," I interrupted. "I was hiding in the *Banelco*. They stopped on another street."

Maya exhaled deeply and said, "Thank God."

"Look, I have got to call my mother. Right away. Please!"

"Yes, of course. She must be worried and upset."

Inside, everything was quiet. I dialed our number, knowing the ringing telephone would frighten her, and she would hesitate to answer, fearing the worst. I caught myself mumbling as it rang, "Please pick up, Mother, pick up."

Thankfully, she answered on the second ring.

Before she could even say *bueno*, I spewed into the receiver. "Mother, I am all right."

"Paul!" she shrieked. "Oh my God, what is happening? Have they arrested you? I am worried sick!"

"I'm all right. Nothing's happened. I went home with a friend, and we were hanging out and lost track of the time, that's all. I'm sorry! I should've left earlier," I said with as much calm bravado as I was able.

She started crying hysterically.

"It's all right, Mother. Stop crying. I am fine. Everything is fine. I am going to stay here with my friend and come home as soon as the sun comes up. I will be home in time to get ready for school. Please, please don't worry."

"Who is this friend?" she asked, sounding more in control, more like her usual self. I made up a story about studying for an upcoming exam, but she interrupted me halfway through my excuse.

"I want to speak to his mother," she insisted.

"It is not anyone you know. Just a kid from school. I will explain tomorrow."

"Paul, are you involved in anything?"

"No, Mother. No. It's just a friend."

With a stern voice, she said, "Then why can't I speak to his mother?"

"Please, Mother, you will embarrass me. I am not a child any more."

"Promise me you will not go out at this hour?" she implored, obviously sniveling.

"Everything'll be all right, Mother," I quickly added, cutting her short. "Calm down."

"Thank God. Thank God, Paul. I couldn't bear it if anything happened to you."

"I know. Please don't worry. Please."

She scoffed, "Of course I am worried."

When I got off the telephone, Maya was putting sheets on the couch. I thanked her and promised to leave as soon as the sun came up.

"Shush," she murmured.

When I was alone, I pulled the blanket over my briefs. But I couldn't sleep. My open eyes stared at the ceiling. I thought about my mother alone at home. I thought about the gym and about Agustin. But most of all, I thought about what happened with Maya earlier that evening and what Maya said about it—how everything was happening here for the first time. I wondered if there was something wrong with me, something unknowable lurking somewhere inside me that made me different from other boys. It was as if I had never really thought about it before.

A toilet flushed somewhere in the building. I heard the sound of sirens in the night, far off but bellowing in the darkness. The floor creaked. I was startled to see Maya standing over me.

"Can't fall asleep?" she asked.

"No."

She said I could sleep with her and led me into the bedroom again.

She must have sensed that my nerves were really rattled. "We're just going to sleep," she said.

"I am sorry. I didn't mean to do that."

"You did a very dangerous thing, Eduardo, for both of us. You must be more careful."

"I know," I replied. Once again, I wondered why things were like this, but I reminded myself that it is best not to discuss these things.

I lay quietly with Maya by my side, absorbed again in my own thoughts. She started massaging my neck and back. "You've had a rough night. Are you sure you're okay?"

Maya's touch was soft, expert and smooth. I felt myself getting aroused. It was uncomfortable lying on my stomach, a growing hard-on wedged under my dead weight. When I rolled onto my back, Maya cuddled next to me and laid an arm across my chest.

"Relax," she said. "You're safe now." Her elbow rubbed up against the bulge pushing against the waistband of my briefs, and she tensed up.

"I'm sorry," I said, thinking that after what I had just put her through, it was kind of weird to have an erection now.

She hesitated for a moment before peeling back the waistband and softly running her hand along my privates, which she cradled the way a boy rolls a handful of marbles.

My instinct was to turn back on my stomach and withdraw into myself. But Maya tightened her grip on my cock and started moving it up and down, occasionally pushing my foreskin all the way back and rubbing the exposed head. In her hands, it got rock hard. She told me to let her know before I came.

"How does it feel?" she asked.

I wanted to say *fantastic,* but I couldn't get it out. I was breathless. My body was quivering. I tried to say I was coming, but it was too late. The forces of nature had taken over, and the surge was gathering within me. The first wave spewed, and then another.

When stillness came, we both laid back, Maya flushed, me limp. The calm bordered on joy.

Maya spoke first. "Do you feel better now?"

"Thank you," I said, breathlessly. "Thank you."

"Let's get some sleep now."

"Do you want me to...?"

"It's okay." She sighed.

*

Maya drew in her arm and turned over, away from me. I sat up carefully. All at once, I felt a sense of emptiness. The excitement of what had just happened was gone. My skin was damp and clammy, and there were still wet spots under the band of my briefs.

Maya was breathing softly, but she wasn't sleeping. After a moment, I asked a question. It was directed as much into the darkness as to Maya.

"Why is it dangerous to be out at night?"

Maya didn't stir, and for a moment, I assumed she might be sleeping after all. Rearranging the pillow on my side of the bed, I burrowed my face deeper into its fold and tried to do the same.

Then Maya spoke—also into the darkness.

"You *must* know this answer," she said with a tone of disbelief.

I told her I wasn't sure and asked why no one talked about it.

There was another long pause—so long that I thought she was going to ignore my question.

"Bad things are happening at certain hours."

"But why?" I asked.

"No one really knows, but there are many rumors. People are taken away because the government suspects they may have information or beliefs that are subversive. Some say they are beaten."

"But what kind of information?" I asked.

"As I said, just anti-government stuff," Maya replied a bit impatiently.

"Do you believe this?"

"I don't know," Maya replied. "They say you can be taken to jail just for having long hair or a beard. For this alone."

"I think it's true," I said. "I read it in a foreign newspaper. Soldiers are arresting people and taking them away."

Maya abruptly sat up and looked at me. "You *do* know or must suspect. How did you see this newspaper?"

"It was in the English newspaper, *The Financial Times*. Sometimes, my mother brings it home from the hotel she works at."

After a long pause, each of us again lying with our backs to the other, deep in our own thoughts, I asked if she knew the word *chupado*.

"No, what is this word?"

I explained it means 'sucked up' and refers to the people who are being taken away.

"Who do you think is doing this? You must have some idea," she asked.

"No one knows. They wear masks. The government says they are from gangs, but the newspaper says they are connected to the military."

After another long pause, Maya told me it was dangerous even to discuss these things and suggested we go to sleep.

I agreed and was about to close my eyes when Maya rolled onto her side and faced me.

"Eduardo," she said, "you should not tell anyone else about those newspapers. Just knowing about them could get you in trouble."

I cannot explain what happened next. But before Maya turned back and resettled into her pillow, I had one final thing to say.

Turning my head toward hers, I said, "Maya, my name is not Eduardo; it is Paul—Paul Casales."

After another long pause, looking straight up at the ceiling, Maya sighed and said, "You must be more careful, Paul."

*

When I awakened in the morning, Maya was already dressed in her starched white nurse's uniform. She was sitting at the kitchen table doing some last-minute prep for her day, which, she explained, consisted of working in one of the clinics beginning in about an hour, followed by classes all afternoon. She offered me a cup of coffee and a shower but told me I would have to hurry. "You can help yourself to some cereal. There's not much else to eat."

I declined the cereal but poured myself a cup of coffee and got into the shower. Maya's cosmetics covered the small shelf above the sink. White nylon stockings were hanging on a makeshift clothesline stretched over the radiator. I lingered under the hot water until my skin was shriveling all over. When I was done, I put my jeans on and stuffed my stained briefs into one of the back pockets. I didn't notice the quiet.

When I returned to the kitchen, it was empty. The kitchen table had been cleared. No books, just a handwritten note. *Please leave as soon as you are done. The door will lock behind you. It is best if we leave things as they are and we don't see each other again.*

I read the note several times and went into the cramped living room. Although I was anxious to return to my own apartment, I sat for a moment on the sofa and thought about what had just happened to me. I comforted myself with the thought that at some point, in a week or so perhaps, last night's events would fade away and be meaningless. I decided to leave a note of my own. *Thank you for last night and for saving me. I understand why you don't want to see me any more. To tell you the truth, I probably would not have tried. Not that I don't like you that way. Just reasons. Paul*

I noticed Maya's full name, Maya Cerdán, on an open utility bill. I copied it and her telephone number on a piece of scrap paper by the phone just in case I changed my mind and put the note in my pocket.

*

Taking advantage of the summer's long twilight hours, I started staying around the gym's café after finishing my workout, sometimes until closing. I liked it most after everyone else had left and it was just Agustin and me. Agustin usually stood quietly behind the counter, reading a book, his elbows on the bar and his head in his hands. Sometimes, he looked up and caught me glancing at him. Mindful that he was supposed to be waiting on the café's customers, and I was a customer, he would ask if I needed anything or smile awkwardly and go on reading.

I had been noticing another kid around my age who had started coming to the gym around the same time as I did. He always arrived with two brothers, one of whom was about two years older and the other no more than twelve. They never deviated from the same routine, walking directly through the café to the locker room, eyes down, pausing just long enough to pick up towels, but otherwise keeping entirely to themselves. When they emerged, each wearing a black Speedo and flip-flops, they went directly to the pool and horsed around for thirty minutes or so. Eventually, the older and younger brothers would leave, but the middle brother invariably stayed behind and swam laps. He was a serious swimmer.

I imagined him as the captain of a high school swim team. His legs and arms opened and closed with the precision of scissors, and his back skimmed the surface of the water, barely disturbing it.

I started timing my workouts so I could grab a few dry towels and settle into one of the chaises around the pool just before he finished his swim. I didn't want to be conspicuous, even though I probably was. I liked watching him hoist himself out of the water. His body was slender and lightly muscled. Dark brown hair, bordering on black and shiny with water, lay flat against his head. Droplets of water ran off his shoulders and down his back.

The boy never deviated from his ritual. He paused at the top of the ladder, hands on hips, his Speedo seemingly molded to his body. As soon as he finished shaking the chlorinated water out of his hair, I knew he would rub the loose water from his shoulders and arms, then his legs, and tug at the front of his bathing suit until it puffed out with air. With a towel wrapped around his waist, he always walked directly to the locker room, a diminishing trail of wet footprints behind him, oblivious to others, including me.

I asked Agustin about him after one of my own workouts.

"Who?" he asked. "Oh, you mean Marco? Nice kid. He's from San Isidro and goes to school at *Nacionale*," Agustin said with an air of respect.

Although *Colegio Nacionale de Buenos Aires* is a public high school, it is the most prestigious in Argentina.

Most of its graduates go on to become leaders in the law, government or science. It was not surprising then that Marco, like Agustin, had a knack for easy conversation. He just walked up to people and started talking, a skill I envied and was determined to learn.

*

Agustin threw me a wet towel and told me to wipe the tables. His informality was a sign that I was now one of the 'regulars'. When I handed back the towel, he reminded me that it was getting late and I should start changing back into street clothes.

"Be quick about it," he ordered. "We need to close up and get home before curfew."

"I'll only be a minute."

I usually avoided the locker room when I knew Marco was changing. I recalled how when I first started attending secondary school the locker room was a place of confusing magnetism, full of exposed boys' bodies that seemed to dare me to look. Tonight, I had no choice. Both Marco and I were running late.

When I entered the locker room, Marco's back was turned. A wet towel lay on the concrete floor under his bare feet. He was pulling up his jeans.

"Hey," he said, and then bent over and started rummaging through his gym bag for his shirt, a frayed *Nacionale* T-shirt with nearly worn-off blue and white letters. When he looked up, he started talking. At first, the conversation was strained. I felt like I was bumbling.

"You must live nearby?"

"Off Corrientes, just a few blocks away," I sputtered.

"I'll remember that. It may come in handy having a friend near this place in case I miss the last bus," Marco said with what looked like a wink.

His reference to me as a 'friend' was both terrifying and gladly received.

"I'll give you my telephone number," I said, trying to sound casual. "Do you have something to write with?"

Marco dug a biro out of this bag and handed it to me.

Pointing to the clock on the wall, he quickly finished dressing and turned to leave, his hair still damp and uncombed. "It'll be dark soon. If I don't get moving, I'll have to call you tonight!"

"What's your family name?" he asked.

"Casales," I responded.

"Bueno. Mine is Campora, Marco Campora."

"You better hurry," I replied, adding *Marco* almost as an afterthought.

"Mañana Casales."

I was still repeating his name when I arrived at my local cafeteria on the corner of Lavalle and Esmeralda, just a block from our apartment. At a table in the window, nursing just a coffee, I replayed in my head everything Marco said. I was in a world apart, oblivious to everything around me: the noise, the bright neon sign on the *farmacia* across the street, the pedestrian traffic outside. When the waiter asked me to finish my coffee and pay, I dropped a few pesos in the dish and briskly walked to the apartment, feeling about as content as I had ever been in my life. My mother was sitting in her usual spot in the living room, absorbed in a book. I wanted to go right to my room and was hoping she didn't feel like talking.

*

I stepped into the living room. The lights were dim, and it felt more claustrophobic than usual.

"Where have you been?" she asked reproachfully.

She signaled for me to sit. Normally, I would. She liked having me around even though we usually sat together quietly. She would keep reading her book, looking up occasionally as though I had said something she missed. I resented how she still treated me as a child.

"I have something for you," she said as I backed out of the room. "There's a couple from Amsterdam staying at the hotel. They brought yesterday's *Herald Tribune*. It says some of the European countries are threatening to boycott the World Cup."

"Let me see it."

"It says the government was involved in Actis' killing."

She was referring to Omar Actis, the head of the World Cup organizing committee who was gunned down on the city streets several months before. The government's official investigation pinned the assassination on opposition guerillas, but no one believed that. In the end, a handful of star players and a few countries made noises about boycotts, but no nation pulled out.

She went on, "There's a big fret about a player named Kreef."

"You mean Cruyff, Johan Cruyff. C-R-U-Y-F-F? He's Holland Total's star forward."

"Well, anyway, he's refusing to play in the tournament."

I shrugged, signaling that she was talking nonsense. Cruyff had won the European Footballer of the Year award three times, but he had yet to win a World Cup. He had just missed out on it three years ago, and Holland was the hands-on favorite to take it next year. There was no way he would miss the tournament. I waved a hand to signal the end of discussing this.

"Do you want something to eat?" she asked. "You must be hungry?"

"Not really. I had a sandwich at the café." I just wanted to be alone in my room where I could again go over this evening's events.

"I am hungry, and *you* need to eat. I waited for you. A sandwich is not enough."

"You eat. I am not hungry. I am going to my room," I replied a bit too sharply.

"Paul," she asked, "what's wrong with you?"

"Mother! You have to leave me alone when I want to be by myself. I am seventeen, practically an adult."

"Do you think I don't know that? Of course, I do, but… What if…?" her voice trailing off.

"Don't say it!" I blurted out. "Nothing is going to happen to me. Okay?"

She frowned. "You don't know that."

"Just eat on your own. Please. I had something to eat at the café after leaving the gym. I am exhausted." I don't think I had ever been as curt with my mother.

*

The next day passed slowly; actually, slower than that. Minutes expanded. I couldn't concentrate and wasn't listening to a word the instructors were saying at school. The only thing I could think about was meeting Marco later that evening at the gym. I arrived before anyone, even Agustin, and took a seat at one of the tables in the lobby. The day trainer had seen me before but didn't know who I was. Marco usually arrived just before four o'clock, but he was late. At my table, I checked my watch and bit my fingernails. I wasn't angry that he was late, but I admit I was hoping he would be early. Wouldn't that have been a signal that he was as anxious to see me as I was to see him?

Regulars came and went, some of whom recognized me and said, "Hey." Agustin arrived shortly after. His blond hair was freshly cut—shorter curls than usual. He walked directly behind the counter and removed a pair of eyeglasses and two schoolbooks from his backpack.

When he saw me, he smiled and came out from behind the counter.

"What's up, Casales?" he asked. "You look puzzled."

"Nothing," I lied.

"Are we going to work out tonight?"

"Uh-hum," I mumbled, slightly embarrassed that I had nothing else to say.

"Grab a couple of towels and get changed," Agustin said as he got up. He always wanted to get started before the after-work crowd took over the weights and machines.

Marco arrived a few minutes later and, as usual, briskly walked through the locker room toward the door to the pool. He hesitated just long enough to drop a gym bag at the foot of his locker. I knew it contained the street clothes he would change into after his workout.

Just as he reached the door, he saw me out of the corner of his eye.

"There you are," he bellowed jovially. "I was wondering why I didn't see you on the way in."

"Hey," I replied, trying to sound totally nonchalant but annoyed that I couldn't think of anything cleverer.

I was expecting and hoping Marco would say something, but he didn't. An uncomfortable silence took hold. It seemed the onus was on me to say something else. If I don't, I thought it would be apparent that I don't have that something that allows both Agustin and Marco to converse effortlessly.

"There were a couple of kids here earlier from *Nationale*," I finally said.

That did it. Marco perked right up. "Oh, who?"

"I don't know. They were taking turns on the treadmill. Agustin will probably know them."

"Thanks," Marco said, "I'll ask him later."

*

When I finished my own workout, I went right to the pool to watch Marco finishing his. Apparently, he was already done. The water was motionless. I followed what was left of wet footsteps into the locker room, went right to my locker, and took a seat on the bench. Marco was not there, either. As my ears adjusted to the silence, I heard the shower. *He's in there*, I thought. I undressed, put a towel around my waist and walked toward the shower room, stopping on the way to use the urinal.

He was there, under a halo of foamy shampoo, facing the wall. After a few seconds, Marco turned around, eyes tightly closed, rivulets of shampoo streaming from his head over his face and down between the solid mounds of his pectorals. He had dark brown nipples, a barely colored thistle of hair between them and a thin trail running down from his navel. His pink-brown penis jutted from a dark mound of pubic hair.

When I looked up, Marco's eyes were open. The expression on his face was blank.

"Hey," he said cordially as he pushed back his hair and wiped the water out of his eyes. Apparently, being seen naked didn't faze him in the least. He did not seem even remotely uncomfortable.

"I thought you had left," I said.

"Yeah, I really am late. I should be out of here by now," he said, a little concerned.

I stepped under the shower head next to his. He lobbed a quick glance at me.

"What's up?" I asked.

"I have to be in San Isidro tonight." He said something about a dinner party his father was hosting, but it didn't fully register.

"How do you get there?"

"The Mitre train. One of my brothers picks me up when it arrives."

"From Estacion Retiro?" I asked, knowing that it was just a short walk.

"Yeah."

"Do you mind if I walk with you," I asked, summoning all of the self-confidence I had at that moment.

"That'd be great. I'll tell you what. My train leaves at six-thirty. There are some cafes on the way. If you have time, we can grab a quick coffee."

"Great. I don't have to be home until curfew."

That apparently settled; Marco turned and leaned headfirst into the spray for a final rinse. With his back turned, I focused on the thin line of brown hair halving his butt cheeks, and although I knew it was not right, I let my eyes linger there a second or two longer than I should. That was the moment I realized I was falling in love with Marco. It was a sensation not like the kind between a man and a woman, but love like the kind he believed existed between men in arms.

*

It is hard to describe what I was feeling when I followed Marco out of the gym. When we reached the bottom of the stairs, he turned and walked in front of me backward. Could it be that he was as happy at the prospect of becoming my friend as I was at becoming his? Surprisingly, and for the first time, the conversation was easy for me. We talked about a lot of things—Agustin, his brothers, swimming. I was right; he was the captain of his school's swim team. More impressively, it turned out he was training for the upcoming Pan American Games.

Marco's train was leaving in less than fifteen minutes. We stood at a counter in a run-down café across from the station, where we could just barely hear the gate and track announcements. I tried to picture Marco's home.

Soon, they announced Marco's train. I wanted to ask if he wanted to hang out again sometime. But I was afraid it sounded too desperate, so I settled on confirming that I would see him at the gym and said I would be looking forward to our next meeting.

*

Maya occasionally thought of that night with 'Eduardo', whom she never got used to thinking of as Paul. She wished he had not returned to her apartment. When she went down to open the door, she knew others in the building had been awakened and imagined still others might be watching them through the closed window shutters up and down Calle Ecuador.

She had just arrived home from a ten-hour shift at the hospital when the cars stopped in front of her building. Within moments, there was a loud knocking on her door, and a gruff male voice ordered her to open it. She was terror-struck but obeyed. Four armed men wearing masks and military fatigues immediately burst into the apartment and took hold of her.

She tried to explain there was some mistake. One of them led her directly into the bedroom. The others were ransacking the kitchen and living room—dishes were breaking, and books and papers were falling to the floor.

"Get dressed!" was the command.

When she returned to the living room, everything had been sacked, with her world practically turned inside out and callously rearranged. With a tight grip on her arm, the soldier pulled and pushed Maya into a dining chair. *This is not—cannot be—happening*, she thought.

The soldier reached down and put a rough hand under her chin, then clamped it around her jaw as tight as a vice grip and pulled her face toward his own. Maya forced herself to look into the eyes, glowering through the holes in his facemask. But she saw nothing, no compassion, no pity—only blackness.

"Give us names."

When she didn't respond immediately, the soldier pulled her even closer. "Speak up. We may not give you another chance," in a voice that seemed as mocking as it did terrifyingly.

Maya twisted but couldn't free her chin from the soldier's grip. Her cheeks were burning.

"No. Please," she whimpered.

The soldier stepped back, made a snorting noise, and then repeated his demand. "Names, bitch!"

Maya tried again to tell him there was some mistake and that she wasn't involved in anything. The soldier didn't respond, didn't even look up at her. He just took a worn notebook out of his chest pocket and ordered Maya to write.

"I don't know who you're looking for," she sniveled.

"Every one of you fucking students knows who we're looking for," he insisted. "Where is your address book?"

"In there."

"Get it!"

Maya slowly backstepped over books and the other possessions on the floor, stumbling once or twice. When she returned to the living room, the soldier grabbed her arm again and pushed her back into the chair.

"Please don't hurt me," Maya moaned as she handed it to him. "I'm trying."

The soldier flipped through the alphabetized pages of her address book, one by one, sometimes turning quickly to the next page and other times pausing as if he recognized a name and was trying to recall where he had seen it before. Every few pages he read out someone's name and asked questions. Between breaths, Maya explained that none of them were really friends, just students in her class with whom she occasionally studied. "If they are involved in anything, I wouldn't know," she added. Maya insisted again that she was being truthful and she wasn't political.

When he reached the end of the book, he asked about a note stuck behind the last page. "Who's Paul?" he asked.

"I don't remember," Maya sputtered. The soldier slapped her. "He is just someone I met one night in a cafeteria."

"What does this mean, 'Other reasons?'"

"I don't know. He was just here for an hour or so."

"Why are you lying to me?" the soldier yelled in her face. "What else?"

"There is nothing else. He was a kid I just met and he came back to my apartment for a while. Nothing else."

"Where does he live?"

"I don't know. I don't. Some place nearby, I think. He walked home."

"And that's it? You never saw him again?"

"No. I mean, 'yes'! I never saw him again."

The soldier paused and, then flipping the pages, started at the beginning again, occasionally asking about other people or going back over the same ones. Sometimes, he wrote something on the pages before turning to the next. When he came to the last page again, he put the book and Paul's note in his pocket and signaled they were through. As the soldiers took one more look around, Maya faintly hoped they would leave. *Please, please, please leave.*

*

The soldiers had other plans. "Take her."

"No!" Maya screamed. Without saying so much as a word, two soldiers yanked her up and, one on each arm, pulled and pushed her toward the door, down the stairs, and out into the night.

Two dark green Falcons were idling in the street, light rain falling in their headlights. The soldiers pushed her into the back seat of the lead car. As soon as the back door shut, one of the men got into the front seat beside the driver. He was quiet for a minute and then shouted, "Go!"

The car leaped onto Calle Ecuador and sped into the dark. As it traveled on Corrientes, Maya turned her body to see where they were going. Everything was blurred by the rain, but she could see well enough to know the other car was close behind, its headlights haloed pale yellow. She tried calming herself, still thinking this would be resolved as soon as she was allowed to explain. *They don't take people away for no reason.*

After what seemed like an eternity, the car slowed and turned onto a dirt road. Maya couldn't tell for sure that it was dirt because she had been blindfolded. But she figured it must be by the way the car bumped and swayed. She also sensed that it was raining harder. Heavy drops were pounding on something metallic, something tinny like the wavy metal sheeting you see in the shanty towns. The pounding stopped just before the car came to a halt. A metal door rattled above. As soon as it locked into place behind the car, they pulled Maya out of the back seat and slammed the rear door. The thud echoed. From the sound of it, she was in some kind of building, maybe a garage.

At first, the soldiers didn't know what to do with her. She was yet to break, but they knew she would *'cause the girl's a fucking student, and we know how to deal with her.'* One of them immediately got in her face. "Out there, you're high and mighty," he shouted. Working himself into a fury. "Yep. Well, I have news for you. Here you're shit, bitch. You're nothing. You no longer exist. We're the mighty ones now."

Before he could finish, another soldier took over. "I'll take it from here," he said with a badge of authority.

But the angry soldier didn't let up. "Don't forget me," he hollered. "Don't forget me, bitch!"

As he was hollering, the man holding Maya's arm tugged her toward him and ordered her to walk. She couldn't.

"I said 'walk,'" he repeated. A firm hand on her shoulder shoved her forward into the nothingness. When Maya didn't move, he pushed harder again. Finally, with arms and hands outstretched like antennae, she took a small step. He pushed again, and she took another step, then another. After several more shoves and twenty or so small steps, each more frightening than the last, the man ordered her to stop. A door opened, and the man shoved her again. Then it closed hard and tight behind her, wood on wood.

For a moment, nothing stirred. Maya wasn't sure if the man had left or was still with her. Then he stepped forward and roughly tugged at her blindfold. When her eyes adjusted to the light, she was terror-stricken. He was pointing a pistol at her head.

"Get on the floor," he ordered.

Maya crossed her hands over her face. "No, no!" she cried, "please don't kill me."

"Down!" he ordered.

"Please, please. Please don't shoot me," she bawled.

"On the floor!" he repeated. Then he said it again slowly. "On… the… floor, now."

She collapsed to the floor, crying uncontrollably.

"Look at me!"

Maya couldn't.

"Look when I say look, bitch!"

Maya covered her eyes and raised her head halfway. She was shaking uncontrollably. "Please… don't… shoot… me," she begged, solely and in a barely audible whisper.

The man suddenly and slowly lowered the gun to his side. "You're going to wish I had." And with that, he turned and left the room.

Four different men replaced him. They were not wearing uniforms, just disheveled street clothes and grimy black masks. Maya could smell stale booze and was sure they were almost, or fully, drunk. She slithered back crablike and curled into a tight ball as the men slowly descended upon her. In no time, her jeans were balled up in a heap at the base of her feet, and her arms and legs were parted.

"Pin the bitch on the table!"

"Please, please don't," Maya pleaded. If she was frightened before, she was horrified now. Yet, her voice was more controlled and clearer than it had been since the start of her ordeal hours earlier. She was resigned to what she knew was coming and hoped it would be over quickly.

*

Morning came. My alarm went off at six thirty, and immediately, I was filled with anticipation. It was the first Wednesday of the month, which meant the school would let out early for one of the junta's monthly student rallies. Attendance was mandatory, not just for my school but for every secondary school within miles of downtown Buenos Aires, including *Colegio Nacionale*, which meant that Marco had to be there as well.

At midday, I settled onto the grass at the far end of the Plaza de Mayo. As forecast, the heat was almost unbearable. Admiral Emilio Massera, the commandant of the Argentine Navy and the most eloquent orator among the junta's senior leaders had already started speaking from the Casa Rosada's balcony. I was a bit surprised by his appearance. Although he was widely regarded as one of the most baleful of the military figures who frequently strutted across that balcony in those days, he was small stature and had a dark complexion which notoriously earned him the nickname of 'El Negro'.

Massera petitioned us to turn away from subversive activities, even subversive thinking, which, in his mind, were one and the same: "Argentina is the theatre of a war that had to be fought against those whose activities—and thoughts—were subversive." He seemed invulnerable to doubt. "To be a sympathizer," he proclaimed, "is the same as being a terrorist."

As I was sitting back down, a woman tapped me on the shoulder. I jumped, hoping for a split second that it was Marco. The woman was standing at my side, wearing an embroidered white scarf and a sad, kindly expression. "Please take this," she said, forcing a piece of paper into my hand.

I was about to say, "no, thank you." But she had already moved on to the boy next to me. He refused the paper as if it was something unclean and glared at me. Following his lead, I balled up the paper in my hand and dropped it.

When I got up to leave, the sun was high in the sky. Some kids had started tossing a frisbee. A part of me wanted to join them, but, as usual, I hesitated. As I was trying to get up the courage to edge my way in, another woman approached. I sensed right away that she was also going to pigeonhole me and turned away. Nevertheless, she also handed me a piece of paper and then asked me to just read it. The way she said it made me curious, so I took cover in the crowd and glanced at it. The single piece of mimeographed paper contained a grainy black-

and-white photo of a young man, probably no older than me. The picture appeared to have been taken at a birthday party. Under the photo, it said: *My son, Lázaro Melchor Obregon.* Under this, typed in clumsy block lettering, it simply said:

LAST 7 APRIL, AT FOUR A.M., THEY TOOK MY SON AWAY, AND I HAVEN'T HEARD ANYTHING ABOUT WHAT MIGHT HAVE HAPPENED TO HIM. THE GOVERNMENT HOUSE SAID THEY COULD NOT TELL ME ANYTHING. THE POLICE SAID IF HE DISAPPEARED SIX MONTHS AGO AND I HAD NOT HEARD FROM HIM, HE WAS DEAD. THIS CANNOT BE TRUE. PLEASE HELP ME FIND MY BOY.

It also said there was going to be a rally the following afternoon in the Plaza de Mayo.

I knew right away that these women were the ones I had read about in one of my mother's bootleg copies of the *International Herald* from the hotel. According to the article, the mothers of these missing persons defiantly met in the Plaza every Thursday in the generals' full view, right under the windows of the Casa Rosada.

Before leaving, I reminded myself that I had gone to the rally hoping to meet Marco. I thought briefly about staying for a while longer, sure Marco would be among the groups of kids still playing in the grass at the far end of the Plaza. But I felt vulnerable standing there alone. It was a strange feeling. I felt like Marco was somehow unaffected and safe from the perils that seemingly were touching me.

*

I didn't know what to do with myself on Thursday. Before I got out of bed, I reached under the mattress and took out the paper I was handed by the woman at the Plaza. I read again what it said and stared at the boy's picture. I lay in bed for a while, wondering what he had done and what my mother would do if something like that ever happened to me.

It was only five-fifteen, so I thought about turning over and trying to get another hour of sleep. But after fifteen minutes, I got up and went to the kitchen, where my mother soon joined me.

"Something is wrong, Paul. What is it?"

"Can I ask you a question?"

"Of course," she responded and sat at the kitchen table.

"Is this why it is dangerous to be out at night?" I asked, nodding toward the open, crumpled paper on the table.

It was instantly apparent that her answer had been rehearsed, as she knew it was inevitable that I would ask.

Sighing deeply, she looked down at her hands and rubbed one against the other, her face suspended between relief and concern. Speaking slowly and deliberately, she explained that the military was searching for certain people. "That's when the security forces are out, at night. There are rumors that anyone can be taken away. Some people never come back. It is unknown where they are.

Their families are looking for them and cannot find them."

"Do you know about these women?" I asked, pointing again to the paper.

"Yes," she said, glancing at the paper and adding firmly. "You don't listen to me, Paul. But where this is concerned, you must. You *must*. I have told you already to stay away from the Plaza de Mayo. I forbid you to go anywhere near these demonstrations. Please promise me you will not."

"But we are required to go to the rallies on Wednesday. I must go to the Plaza. Why stay away from these women in white or any other, as you call, demonstrators?"

"Because I don't want you involved in any kind of politics. As long as we aren't involved in anything, we have nothing to fear. If we don't question, we won't be stopped, and no one will come. You must do this for me. I could not bear it if anything was to happen to you. Do you understand?"

Dutifully, I said I did. But, in truth, I still had many questions, and I resented, again, being treated as a boy.

"Paul, you must not take risks. It is dangerous. You must mind your own business and not get involved in anything," she said directly into my eyes.

*

The Plaza de Mayo was just twelve blocks from my school, a fifteen-minute walk by the most direct route.

That Thursday, after school got out, I found myself walking in that direction. I was not sure what I was thinking. But I was conscious of the fact that I was deliberately disobeying my mother, something I was unaccustomed to and uncomfortable doing. I wondered whether that was part of a larger rebellion against her authority or just a sign that I was ready to start making some decisions for myself.

The Casa Rosada stretches the Plaza's entire width on its east side. It is the headquarters of the junta. It is the reason most people, like my mother, avoid it. It is best known for the balcony from which Juan Péron rallied his supporters in the 1940s, and his wife, Evita, famously declined the nomination to become the nation's vice-president and announced that she had cancer, which would take her life months later. In 1982, the regime's third and final military president, General Leopold Galtieri, appealing to blind nationalism and crude chauvinism, used the historic balcony to harangue a crowd in support of the Falklands/Malvinas War. A few short months later, he returned to the same balcony to announce Argentina's humbling rout by the British.

I paused at the corner of Hipólito Yrigoyen and surveyed the crowded rectangular square in front of me. My eyes immediately traveled to the white obelisk in its center and the white marble statute that capped it, a woman in flowing white robes clutching a spear, her face fixed on the opaque windows of the Casa Rosada. I wondered who or what she was intended to symbolize and whether the generals realized she was watching everything they did.

Approximately fifty women were walking in a slow, solemn procession around the obelisk's base, each wearing a white headscarf with sky-blue lettering. I subsequently learned of the scarves' origin and significance: the generals banned public protests—loosely defined as groups carrying placards or making a public speech. The mothers did not want to deliberately court arrest. On the contrary, their cause might be forgotten if too many of them were incarcerated. So, they adapted. Instead of speeches, they marched silently, and instead of placards bearing the names and photographs of their missing loved ones, they embroidered their loved ones' names and the date of their disappearances onto their white headscarves, which proved to be a moving demonstration. The mosaic of their scarves became a living, moving quilt of sorrows.

When I crossed to the Plaza, I moved closer to the march in a series of advances, each time taking shelter behind one of its many large *Palo Barracho* trees. As soon as I was safely behind one tree and satisfied the path was clear, I moved to the next one until, finally, I was close enough to gaze directly into a few of the mothers' eyes. I realized they didn't have to deliver speeches or carry placards. Their cause was etched in their faces, just as the *Herald* had said.

I thought of the boy in the picture. His name was emblazoned in my mind: Lázaro Melchor Obregon. I surveyed the promenade and tried to imagine which of the women was his mother. That's when I realized soldiers on horseback were assembling nearby. Their shiny silver and blue helmets were clearly visible. The horses' hooves were clopping on the paving stones, a sign they were getting ready to move and break up the assembled crowd. *That was enough for one day,* I thought. I had seen what I had come to see.

I left immediately, recalling my mother's warnings, relieved to once again be among the anonymous people on the sidewalk, assuming there was such a thing in our city in those times. Calamitous noise soon started coming from the direction of the Plaza, and for the next hour, frightened men and women passed by, each carrying his or her own rage. The thing I will always remember about that scene was the bond between these people on the one hand and, on the other, the detachment of the shopkeepers and government workers who watched the march from a safe distance. There may have been a hint of concern in some of the peoples' eyes, perhaps even sympathy, but most did not appear to feel any compassion for those silent women. So long as it was not personal, it seemingly had no effect on them. My mother's words, "Don't look at anything."

*

Marco and I were meeting regularly at the gym and spending more time together. When my mind wasn't on schoolwork, it was on him. He was becoming a real friend. Or should I say, he was becoming what I thought of as a real friend? I had not known another. We met every Monday, Wednesday and Thursday and pretty much locked into a routine. The first one to arrive would wait in the lobby for the other, usually making small talk with Agustin. When the other arrived, the two of us went right into the locker room and changed Marco into a bathing suit and me into a sweat suit. As we closed and locked our lockers, we made plans to meet up and shower after our workouts. Most often, I walked Marco back to school or to the train station, depending on whether he was staying that night, usually stopping for coffee along the way.

With Marco out of town on weekends, the days passed slowly. He spent the time in San Isidro, where I imagined he had other friends in addition to his brothers. I wondered if he missed our workouts—actually me—as much as I missed our comradery.

When there was nothing else to do, most of the time, I sat quietly with my mother, usually catching up on homework or reading a book. Our relationship was changing. She seemed to be loosening the reins a bit, except where politics was concerned. She still did not stop reminding me of the danger of 'getting involved'.

On one particular Saturday evening, we were sitting at the kitchen table. I was picking at leftover *carbonada* when the telephone rang on the small table in the living room. Neither of us was expecting a call, so we both sat still for an instant, listening to it ring, assuming the other would get up to answer it.

"It's probably the hotel," I said.

She nodded and lifted the receiver, *"Bueno."*

After a pause, she said, "Well, I am not sure. May I ask who is calling?"

She paused again, during which I could hear a barely audible baritone voice leaking from the receiver. "I am quite certain my son doesn't know anyone named Campora. May I ask why you are calling?"

"Mother! It's Marco, my friend."

For a second, my heart stopped. Marco had never called me before. I had almost forgotten that I gave him my telephone number. I jerked the receiver from my mother's hands. He spoke right up in his usual light-hearted voice.

"Hola. Que pasa, Paul?" At first, he said he was sorry that he wasn't at the gym on Thursday (he had left me waiting without an explanation) and said that he had exams he had forgotten to tell me about.

Marco then said, "I am hanging out here with nothing to do. If you think you could stand a day in the suburbs, how about coming to San Isidro tomorrow? Spend the night. You can stay in my room. There's space." I felt a surge of exhilaration. He was offering his friendship and a break from the monotony of this small apartment.

I said, "Hey, that's great, even though I knew it was going to be hard to convince my mother to let me go. Really, what else would I say?

My mother was hovering close by, her eyes suspicious, her jaw set tightly. "What's great?" she demanded, and then, immediately checking her tone, she said, "What was that all about?"

I explained how I met Marco and that we had become friends, and he invited me to come to San Isidro for the night. I told her I met Marco at the gym, that Marco was a champion swimmer (even though he had never admitted it), that he went to *Colegio Nacionale*, and that his family lived in San Isidro.

Apparently not listening to what I had just said, she asked, "How did he get our telephone number?"

"I gave it to him," I blurted before I stopped to think how my mother would react.

"I have told you not to give anyone our telephone number. Ever," she scolded. "Don't you know what could happen?"

"You keep saying that you want me to have friends," I sassed back.

"I do, but…"

"But what? How can I have friends if I can't give them my telephone number?" I was taking no pains to hide my irritation.

"Calm down, Paul. I do want you to have friends, but I also want you to be careful. I worry when you are out alone or with people I've never met."

"You suspect everyone," I said, "and want me to do the same. And by the way, I am not alone when I am at the gym."

I knew that, in her own way, she was looking out for me. She feared that anytime I emerged from the isolation of the apartment, I was exposing myself to danger.

"These days, you must go about carefully," she added. "You must watch out."

"Why?" I asked. "I'm not involved in anything."

"No debes ser por algo," she said, straining to stay calm. "You don't have to be involved in anything. Sometimes it doesn't matter."

After taking a deep breath and regaining her composure, she explained how she read in the foreign newspapers that when the military went to a house to arrest someone, if they found an address book, they'd go after the people in it just for being an acquaintance. It was guilt from mere association with others who themselves may have been singled out. I was tired of hearing this and told her so. Marco's family didn't seem concerned with these things.

Sounding resigned to the inevitable, she asked what I knew about Marco. "Have you met his family?"

I said that I had met his brothers at the gym. I added that I thought his family was rich.

"They've got to be rich," she insisted in a tone bordering on contempt. "You have to be rich to live in San Isidro."

She asked what Marco's father did and whether he was involved with the military, for example. I said that I knew only that Sr. Campora held a high position in a government ministry. I didn't know if he was involved with the military. Marco seldom talked about his father except to say that he was always home.

"I'll bet his parents are very nice," I said. "It makes me angry and sad that you distrust everyone."

"I just don't want you getting involved with the wrong people," she explained again how much she resented the military wives when she and my father lived on the military base and how they were so haughty, self-indulgent and contemptuous of everyone not of their status. She reiterated how she wanted something different for me.

When she was talked out, I returned to the subject of Marco's telephone call. I acknowledged her fears but explained that I wanted friends and that Marco had become my best friend. I assured her that he was not an elitist and she would like him.

"Why haven't you brought him around, then?" she asked.

I didn't have an answer, but I promised that I would invite him to the apartment sometime soon if she would let me go to Marco's tomorrow. She looked worried and defeated. She would much prefer that I made friends closer to home, she said. But if I really wanted to go, I could. I had to promise her that I would be careful and not say anything to the Camporas that might be misinterpreted.

"Like what?" I asked sardonically.

*

An austral sunrise over Buenos Aires, particularly in December, the month of the solstice, is unlike the sunrise others are accustomed to. Just a few hours after the day's bright sun widens and finally sets, changing the evening sky to the color once described by someone as 'a sad gold', the first light reappears on the eastern horizon beyond the River Plate. Initially veiled by morning clouds, the rising sun transforms the sky into a fresh patchwork of dull white and lavender. When it breaks out, it sets the thrushes in the city's gargantuan rubber trees scuttling noisily from branch to branch and illuminates the tops of the tallest buildings as if they are sheathed in gold. I awoke to just such a morning that Saturday.

Estacion Retiro's great hall was eerily quiet at seven o'clock. I had never seen it without long lines and the tempest of arriving and departing passengers fighting to get through the turnstiles at the end of the platforms. But at this hour, the only sounds were the muffled echoes of the few patrons' footfalls on the floor tiles. A dull green light bulb marked the single open ticket window on the far end of the island in the center of the great hall. Except for a few cafes, the kiosks were still shuttered. When the gravelly loudspeaker broke the silence to announce the boarding of my train, it sounded as if God himself was speaking.

Soon after the train left the station, I leaned back and closed my eyes, imagining the day ahead with a combination of excitement and anxiety. As the train gained speed, I pictured Marco's parents and wondered what they would think of me, if they would like me. Soon, we were passing a crowded, colorless shanty town cobbled together from concrete blocks, cardboard boxes, scraps of metal sheeting and various other scavenged materials. Children ran along the tracks, raising a film of fine dust in their wake. Though ragged, they seemed as frantic and content as children anywhere. Looking back, I recall thinking briefly about their lives and the plight of the other people living in these slums, whose life or death was of no consequence to anyone but themselves.

For the rest of the trip, I thought about what lay ahead. I kept my eyes closed, subconsciously counting off the remaining stops. When the train slowly entered the San Isidro station, I could see Marco and Juan, his younger brother, leaning against the side of the family's Peugeot, sun glinting off the car's windows. Marco's older brother, Santiago, was behind the wheel.

As I approached the car, Santiago turned off the motor and joined his brothers. This was the first time I had seen them all together outside the gym. Standing like that, Santiago, Marco and Juan, in that order, they looked more alike than usual, each a variation on the family mien of dark mahogany hair, deep blue eyes and high Campora cheekbones. Each, in his own way, was a mirror reflection of his parents.

Santiago was the intellectual and his father's favorite. He was thoughtful, private, and less verbose than Marco but not quiet either. Unapologetically handsome, respectful, sensitive and pure of heart, Marco was his mother's favorite and the one to whom she turned when she needed consoling. Juan was five years younger than Marco and, so, 'the baby'. By the time Juan was born, Santiago and Marco were already attending primary school. Juan was neither the family intellectual nor champion, those roles had already been filled by Santiago and Marco, respectively. But, like his brothers, he was attractive and also was the most spirited. His father always said Juan would never want for friends because he had a breezy, contagious temperament, which often is a trait of the youngest.

If I had not come to know as much about Marco as I already did, I would have assumed that his good looks afforded many privileges on the wings of which he would breeze easily through life. Yet, one of Marco's most endearing qualities, which his brothers also seemed to share, was his seeming lack of narcissism or, at least, that's how he appeared to me then. He was starting to wear his hair on the longish side, constantly falling into his eyes, and he unconsciously brushed it back into place along the top and side of his head with a stroke of his open palm, a motion intended simply to get it out of his eyes rather than to put it back into place. Although I was accustomed to seeing him in his school uniform or a Speedo, standing there in baggy cargo shorts, a Club Atlético T-shirt and flip-flops, he seemed even more self-assured than he did when he was at the gym.

"Welcome to the 'burbs!" Marco hollered as soon as I was within hearing distance. We embraced, and he kissed my cheek. In turn, I kissed Santiago and then Juan.

*

The area of San Isidro where the Camporas lived was one of the most affluent and attractive places I had ever been in my life. Its calm and irregular streets were dotted with open spaces and huge groves. Green was seeping, little by little, back into the lawns; well-ordered flower beds were in bud, and its old trees had recently come into full leaf. On the Camporas' street, expensive houses, each surrounded by gardens, peered over high stone walls and sweet-smelling hedgerows.

What I had heard and imagined about San Isidro prepared me to be impressed, but I was not prepared for the house itself. It was situated sideways, turning a brick end-wall with two leaded glass windows to the tree-lined street. On both sides of the entrance were large dormered wings designed in the Tudor style, all exposed wood beams encased in brick, steeply-pitched slate roofs, and deeply recessed leaded glass windows framed in tangled ivy. The property was surrounded by a high brick wall that dipped low enough between evenly spaced columns to offer glimpses of the prosperity within. Ornate iron gates protected both ends of the curved gravel driveway.

*

I expected Marco's parents to be imposing, bordering on imperial. I knew from Marco that Sr. Campora—Señor Miguel Campora—held an important ministry job and Sra. Campora was a woman with strong convictions. When we finally met, however, I was not surprised. Although slightly graying and not as tall as I imagined, Sr. Campora exuded athleticism and was ruggedly handsome. Sra. Campora, whom Sr. Campora referred to as *Mother*, also was smaller than expected but as dignified and reserved as I was told to expect. She clearly was the source of the boys' complexion and features. She smiled with ease, and it was immediately obvious that she was comfortable and confident in her place in the world. Many people would have been unnerved by what unfolded in front of me, but I was more captivated than nervous. I could not, but did try to imagine what it would be like to be part of a family like theirs.

Immediately after the parental introductions, each followed by kisses on alternating cheeks, Sr. Campora asked me about 'my people'. *What a funny expression,* I thought, *my people.*

"My family?"

"Yes, son," he said. "Tell me about your parents and siblings."

"My father died a few months before I was born. I have lived all my life in Microcentro with just my mother," I said, thinking I had just summed up my seventeen years in two sentences.

"You are an only child?"

"Yes."

"That is hard, no?"

I had never really considered my life quite that way and wasn't sure how to reply. I sometimes wondered what it would be like to have a brother, especially an older one.

"No," I replied, "but sometimes I think it would be nice to have brothers, I guess, you know, like Marco."

"It also must have been hard for your mother, raising you all alone."

"Yes."

"May I ask how your father died?"

"He was a military officer. There was an accident during a training exercise."

"I am sorry."

"Thank you."

"You must be very proud of him being a military officer and all," Sr. Compora said with almost an air of pride himself and an expectation that I would agree.

"Actually, I never knew him… but I suppose so."

"I am sure he was a fine man," Sr. Campora said as his gaze on me steadied.

I was trying so hard to pay attention to his father's questions that I didn't even realize Marco had broken off. I was starting to understand why he warned me about meeting his parents. Did Sr. Campora interrogate all of Marco's friends like this? It was doubtful. There was something unsettling in his questions as if I had to be assessed for acceptability.

"Enough," Sra. Campora finally said. "The boy will think we are meddling."

She had come to my rescue.

*

We had time to kill before lunch, which, I was informed, would be on the lawn at their country club just a short drive from the house. Santiago drove. When we arrived,

Marco led me through the clubhouse's main entrance and into an empty, dusty, dark-paneled room furnished with calfskin rugs, heavy leather furniture, polo gear and various trophies and cups. At eye level, the walls were filled with plaques listing the names of the club's annual champions, some engraved onto thin brass nameplates that had been nailed in neat columns and rows, others painted on. I passed the plaques for rugby, polo and various other sports before spotting the ones for swimming. When I saw on one of the plaques that Marco had been the club champion in the two-hundred-meter crawl for three years running, I was not surprised. I looked at the blank space below the last plate, where I supposed a fourth brass plate would probably be inscribed with his name.

 Sra. Campora joined us while Sr. Campora was speaking privately with Santiago. She was wearing a white linen dress with fresh lipstick, and her black, heavy hair was pulled into a tight bun. Sr. Campora immediately terminated his conversation and proceeded to his wife's side, kissing her dutifully. We slowly made our way toward the lawn in a single file under a large flag swaying listlessly from high on a freshly painted white pole. Its gold-threaded sun was almost as bright as the real one. The Club's ensign drooped motionlessly just beneath it. As we passed the clubhouse, I caught sight of my own image in one of its expansive windows, and for a moment, I imagined what it might be like to belong there. As if reading my mind, Marco draped an arm across my shoulder and smiled.

The 'lawn' was an outdoor patio surrounded on three sides by shoulder-high glass panels in teak frames. It sat under the shade of a majestic banyan tree whose lower boughs were twisted like a Chinese dragon. In some places, the limbs were incapable of bearing their own weight and were held aloft with wooden braces. The tree's pear-shaped leaves might as well have been a tiled roof because very little sun made it through except around the edges. Invisible thrushes chirped their bright music in the branches higher up and occasionally leaped from one to the other.

The little light that did manage to reach through the tree stippled white tables and chairs in neat rows under its canopy. Every table was full, and each man and woman had a drink in hand. It was a portrait of those who are comfortably assured. At the center, the cooks were busily attending to a large *asado*, slabs of dripping meat cooking on poles leaning at various angles over a pile of glowing charcoal. The smell made me even hungrier. Finally, for I was starving, we were shown to our table and stood while the host held back a chair and Sra. Campora gracefully sat. Like the subjects of a queen, each of us then filled in the seats around her, Sr. Campora on her left and Santiago on her right. Sr. Campora immediately signaled to a waiter for the 'usual' cocktails for him and his wife and today's *aqua fresca* for the rest of us.

The two hours we spent at lunch filled us up and made us lethargic, so Marco and I decided to walk back to the house. I was happy to be out of Buenos Aires and away from my mother and in this world so new to me.

"Your parents are very nice," I said, followed by, "what's your father like?"

Marco ran his fingers through his hair, which was, again, in his eyes, flicked his head, and put his hands in his pockets.

"You know, typical Argentinian father. He's the head of the household; it's an absolute. You've probably figured out he was a military officer. I think he misses that. Sometimes, it feels like he never left it. You know, the military."

"How come?"

"Because he is so regimented. Like once a year, he has an elaborate garden party that centers on him gallivanting with military brass. General Agosti himself sometimes comes. You have to be careful what you say around Father. He hates liberals, just hates them."

"Why?"

"He thinks they are all nihilists bordering on terrorists and, of course, bad for Argentina. He is against everything he feels they represent, such as leftism, agnosticism, lawlessness."

"Really?"

"Yeah, really. If he had not gone into the military, he might have become a politician. It seems that he peppers every conversation with an excuse to use words like patriotism, duty, and sacrifice.

"Anyway, you'll see. He will probably call us to the library before dinner for one of his what's-happening-to-Argentina talks. Be ready."

*

Sure enough, when we arrived at Marco's home, there was a note on his bedroom door. Marco read the note and then handed it to me. His father wanted to see us in the library. "Uh-oh, here it comes," Marco murmured. When we entered the room an hour later, my stomach turned to mush. I didn't know what to expect.

The library was a paneled, book-lined room with what appeared to be thousands of serious-looking volumes, from what I could tell, mostly on history, economics and the military. Several heavily stuffed and upholstered sitting chairs were arranged around a coffee table covered with newspapers and magazines and a large mahogany desk at which sat Sr. Campora under a stern portrait whose surface was cracked like ice, an ancestor I presumed. Although cozy, it was not one of Marco's favorite places. He referred to it as his father's sanctum.

After some small talk, mostly about the upcoming World Cup and Pan American games, Sr. Campora became more specific and personal and asked whether Marco was taking good care of me.

"Marco is a good boy," he said. "Sometime soon, we are going to have to decide on a career for him."

Marco looked uncomfortable being talked about like this. But he nodded dutifully.

"And how about you, young man? What are your plans?" The interrogation was back but with no Sra. Campora to change the topic.

I told him how my mother hoped I eventually would attend university. I anticipated the next question and scrambled for an answer Sr. Campora would approve.

"University?" He let the question hang in the air. "What field do you plan to go into? Do you intend to follow in your father's footsteps?" Marco shot me a worried glance. I thought about my mother's antipathy toward the military. It occurred to me then that I had always assumed her opinions were justified but also that I had not formed my own on the subject.

I copped out. "Actually, sir, I haven't decided; I still have another year of school." What else could I say— "My mother wants me to be anything but a military officer?"

Sr. Campora turned a look toward Marco that I could not see, and then gazed back at me.

"Are you considering a military career?" he asked bluntly.

I hesitated for a split second as I put together my answer. The silence was uncomfortable. I could tell Marco was squirming in his seat, and I hoped he would come to my rescue as his mother had. He did not.

"Actually, I am not sure that's an option right now. My mother doesn't have anyone else, only me, so it would be hard always moving from place to place."

"I suppose," he said dismissively. Silence hung as heavy as the ancestral portrait.

Marco caught his father's eye. "Father, I would like to show Paul the swimming pool." Sr. Campora looked down and thought about that for a minute. Without looking up, he murmured something and coolly waved a backhand—apparently our cue that we were dismissed.

Marco immediately motioned me toward the plate glass door that led to the garden. "Come on," he said. I was only too eager to follow!

*

Santiago knocked on Marco's door and informed us that dinner was ready, and we were to go directly to the dining room. Marco had told me in advance that the family usually dressed for dinner, so I put on a pressed white shirt and my best linen pants, both of which were slightly wrinkled from being in the backpack I had brought with me. We walked through several dark-paneled rooms on our way to the dining room. In keeping with the rest of the main house, it was cozy and intimidating in a way that I could not quite identify. Everything seemed too large: sumptuous drapes, huge fading carpets, a cavernous fireplace, heavy wood moldings and a grand table. The table was set at one end for only four. My heart and confidence sank a bit because Santiago and Juan would not be joining us. They had friends visiting with whom they would be eating later in the kitchen. So, it was to be an intimate quartet.

We assembled there at eight o'clock, early by Argentine standards. Sr. Campora ordered drinks for him and Sra. Campora and signaled for us to sit. She had changed into a long red skirt—light and flowy in the flamenco style. A female server dressed in a plain white starched uniform bobbed (something between genuflected and curtsied) and left. I glanced at Marco and imagined we were brothers, especially at this moment.

After we settled into our chairs, Sra. Campora asked about my mother. I was half-expecting another grilling from Sr. Campora and was surprised when she spoke first. I told her how my mother's mother died young, her father had been a bookseller, she had been studying literature when she met my father, and that she still did a lot of reading. I added that she was devoted to me. Sra. Campora nodded kindly. She seemed to like that.

Sr. Campora asked if I also enjoyed reading. "I do," I said, adding that I did not have a lot of time for it with my studies and all.

"What do you like to read?" he asked.

I froze. I didn't know how to answer him. I figured the right answer was military history. But I was not accustomed to lying and not very good at it. And that answer would not square with our earlier conversation.

Fortunately, Sra. Campora immediately changed the subject. Either she could tell from my expression that I was straining for an answer, or she was concerned with where the question might be leading. I wasn't sure.

Eventually, silence took hold. Sr. Campora took a long sip of his drink and lit a cigarette. I looked down and repositioned the napkin on my lap. Mercifully, the pantry door opened, and the server wheeled in a trolley carrying the meals.

Gratefully, small talk took over while we ate.

The server returned to clear the plates and to offer fresh ice cream as the dessert.

While we were waiting, Sr. Campora turned his focus on Marco and asked how school was going and inquired about several of his instructors, several of whom Sr. Campora appeared to know well, even though he, himself, had not attended *Nacionale*. He reminded Marco that it would not be long before *they* had to start thinking seriously about college applications. Then, the conversation turned back to me.

Sr. Campora asked, "Do you two realize how fortunate you are to be living in the capital during these times?"

"I am not sure what you mean, sir," I replied, apparently wrongly.

"There's a war on, son. The stakes are high. Buenos Aires is the principal battlefield on which we are fighting for nothing less than the essence and future of Argentina."

"Oh, Miguel," Sra. Campora interrupted warily. I could not tell if she disapproved of the subject matter or the reasoning or knew this to be a prelude to a speech.

"Mother," Sr. Campora replied. "You know I am right."

Sra. Campora—*Mother*—sat back silently, and Sr. Campora continued, "The bombings, kidnappings and other terrorist acts will soon be history, and the capital will soon enough regain the grandeur of its past. Paul, your train passed the *villas miserias*, the slums along the track, did it not? They have no place in the capital and will soon be bulldozed. Graffiti and other filth must be eliminated, and the 'slum dwellers' along with them. These vagrants must be rounded up. It is a privilege to live in the capital. Those degenerates will have no place in the *new* Argentina! Buenos Aires is and will be for proper people." His oration went on for what seemed like an uncomfortable forever, but likely really was only a couple more minutes.

I cleared my throat and asked what would happen to the people who lived in the *villas* if their homes were to be bulldozed. Trying to sound like I had actually given the subject some thought, I added that I realized many people think they are illegal and ugly and conceded the point. But I also added that I didn't think, somehow, it was all right to bulldoze people's homes.

"Where will they go?" I asked, explaining how my mother raised me to consider the less fortunate.

"Let Paraguay have them," his father said with a nonchalance that sounded callous. I looked over at Marco. He looked back blankly as if this conversation was not happening, or maybe he was not even in the room.

"I asked you earlier, son if you were contemplating a military career," he said, his eyes once again holding mine. "I think you should. It will rid you of these ideas for which there is no place in our society any more. You simply cannot change the order of the way things are.

The war is long overdue, and you need to get into step with it." His grave voice had a triumphant tinge. For the first time, I thought I saw a tiny smile on his face.

Sra. Campora finally broke the tension. "Enough of this talk, Miguel. Let the boys eat their dessert." With that, she lightly pushed my arm as though I required some assistance to get started.

*

Marco and I were finally excused from the dining room table. Sr. Campora immediately went to his study, and eventually, Sra. Campora retired to her room. When Marco and I entered the family room, the evening had aged. Long shadows were stretching across the muted colors of the carpets and the previously gleaming hardwood floors. Marco wanted to talk about his father.

He revealed intimacies that I felt grateful to be hearing. He admitted that he had always known people thought his father had connections in the government because he'd been given an important job in the Mecon, the *Ministerio de Economia y Producción.* The rumors had logic because Sr. Campora wasn't born into an important family and he didn't even have an academic degree. The job had something to do with approving foreign investments in Argentina. The way Marco explained it, his father knew how 'the game' was played, and he played it well, which is to say he knew how to get things done, and he did. Marco told me when he was younger; he occasionally got into fights with classmates who said they'd heard from their parents that Sr.

Campora was a Perónista and a *noquis*—a ghost employee who draws lucrative paychecks from the state-owned enterprises. "Those things aren't true," Marco insisted. "He just has a knack for making friends with influential men. He loves Argentina and wants what's best for our future."

After a long pause, I asked, "Do you want to serve in the military?"

"Not really," he answered, avoiding my eyes and looking down.

"Do you want to go to college?"

"Yeah, I do. I want to study journalism, but my father—well, you saw, you know. He expects and is pushing me into a civil service career like his own."

"Like father, like son?" I asked facetiously.

"Now that you've met him, do you really think I have a choice?"

"But why journalism?"

"I just like government studies, how things happen and all, and have always wanted to be a reporter. My teachers say I am a good writer."

"Do you write for the student newspaper?"

"Oh, no! My father won't let me. He thinks all student newspapers are run by subversives."

*

We retired to Marco's room just after midnight. Although we had been there briefly when I arrived, this was the first opportunity I had to really take it in. It was exactly as I had pictured it so many times in my mind. Like mine, it contained the usual stuff: a team picture of Argentina's Olympic swimmers, posters from some fútbol clubs, newspaper clippings about Marco's swimming victories and taped-up photos of Marco and his brothers. Swimming trophies dotted his bureau and windowsills. Through the window, I could see a half-moon.

My teeth were brushed, and my face washed; I left the bathroom and turned off the light. When I re-entered the bedroom, Marco reminded me that the house was fitted with various security alarms. "If you need to leave the room, you must wake me first."

I woke up in the middle of the night. The room was hushed. The windows were partly open, and the room was washed in faint moonlight. I felt safe. I glanced over at Marco. He was asleep on top of the sheets. He was shirtless, wearing only his pajama bottoms. I wondered what he had looked like as a child. Didn't Sra. Campora say earlier that evening that he was odd-looking until he was about ten.

I quietly approached the side of his bed. His sleep was heavy, with breath soft and rhythmic, his abdomen slowly rising and falling. A small tuft of hair protruded from his waistband. As my eyes settled there, a wave of desire spread through me. I didn't know what I would say if Marco woke up. But I lingered. There was no question. I thought love might be like this.

I had an urgent desire to touch his lips, a nipple, that tuft of hair. Does this make me queer, I wondered? But my denial was equal to my desire. For a moment, I went over my emotional life. I masturbated daily, sometimes thinking of boys, including Marco and Agustin, but only sometimes. Two years ago, I fantasized for weeks about that boy who spent the summer with his grandmother in the apartment next to ours. But then, there was my night with Maya, my first and only sexual experience. *I can't be queer, right? Queer men are effete and effeminate, and that's not me.* My visit to San Isidro had opened a door much larger than the front gate of the Campora home.

My mind was racing when I returned to my own bed. I could hardly keep up with the many emotions stirring up: satisfaction bordering on elation followed as day followed night with the usual confusion, shame and regret. I supposed that all boys fantasized, including me. Yet, I did not think I was fantasizing. What I was experiencing was something different. It was beautiful.

*

For weeks after, I thought about that night with Marco. When we were not at the gym, we were walking side by side, or talking in one of the convenient cafes. One evening in early March, I told him about the mothers who met in the Plaza de Mayo and my mother's reaction to my going there.

After my recounting and a long pause, he agreed that something was wrong in the capital. He asked if I was afraid to go out after dark. I told him about the night I was with Maya, had lost track of the time, and my frightening experience on the Avenida Corrientes. He listened intently to every word as though I was revealing a state secret. He wanted to know if I had ever seen the security forces taking someone away. I said no, not right before my eyes, but that I had seen Falcons in the neighborhood and occasionally heard them screech to a stop, which, I assumed, meant that something was happening.

"What's the big deal?" Marco said, not really as a question. "Bad people get arrested all the time."

"I think this is different," I said, "it's not the regular police. No one seems to know who's doing it. People are taken away during the night by men who do not identify themselves, and when the families go to the police for information, they say they have no record of an arrest. It's like the person just vanished. No one seems to have any knowledge of anything."

"How do you know that?" Marco asked, this time as a real question.

Without thinking, I referred to the foreign newspapers. As soon as that came out of my mouth, I wished I had not said it.

"Have you seen—read—these newspapers?" Marco said in a stern tone.

"Not really," I lied, for the first time seeing Marco as the pride of a conservative upper-class upbringing. "Sometimes I overhear foreigners in my mother's hotel talking about them." I tried to sound as detached from my risky confession as I could.

*

A short while later, Marco told me the Camporas were planning a big party and invited me to come. Most of the guests would be colleagues of his father's, he said, but each of the boys could invite a friend.

In the days before the party, Marco warned me that the party itself would be terribly boring. It would be attended by a lot of cocksure men and their supercilious wives milling around with cocktails and talking softly, smugly. "We will find a way to have fun, though," he assured with a smile.

The night before the party, I carefully packed my same long pants and a white shirt, this time adding a tie. I wanted to look my best, although I suspected it would be apparent to anyone who even glanced at me that I was not of their class. As I applied a fresh coat of polish to my good shoes, I was thinking about Agustin and imagining how he would dress and act. I wished he was coming, too.

The evening of the party was unusually hot for late March. As cars arrived, a uniformed valet took the guests' keys. Sr. and Sra Campora, dressed formally in white linen, stood just inside the door, welcoming each guest and indulging their comments about the heat. Additional servants who had been hired for the evening directed them to the garden where, earlier that day, groundskeepers had strung white lights from tree to tree and set tables on the grass. Several guards milled about. Men in white coats passed food and wine. The men were all smoking either a cigarette or a cigar. A small ensemble played light music.

When Marco and I arrived, the party was well underway. We came down from his room late to avoid the introductions and intentionally stood apart from the clusters of well-dressed men and their wives milling about. I spotted Santiago coming toward us. The heat notwithstanding, he was wearing a dark suit and tie and looked very business-like. He reminded Marco that *we*—meaning Juan, Marco and himself—were expected to socialize, not just stand around together. Perhaps that is why Juan and Santiago had not invited friends. With that, Santiago gestured toward a woman standing by herself. Marco shrugged and dutifully walked over.

A middle-aged man approached and introduced himself to me. Unlike Sr. Campora, he was short and overweight. He was some kind of an executive with a Brazilian bank. When it became apparent that I knew nothing about international banking, or much about Brazil for that matter, he took a long drag on his cigarette, politely excused himself and moved on. That's more or less how the evening proceeded. Guests would introduce themselves, more or less, and tell me how they knew Sr. Campora and drifted away as soon as it was apparent that I was just a schoolboy friend of Marco. Everyone seemed to have a business reason for being there.

Marco introduced me to a Sr. Nestor Benitez, and then was swept away by a group of women sitting at a nearby table. I marveled at Marco's ability to take it all in.

Sr. Benitez, a short and portly man with waxed silver hair, had something to do with the Argentine national oil conglomerate, *Yacimientos Petroliferos Fiscales*. Like so many others, he immediately asked how I was connected to the Campora family. When he learned that I traveled from the Estacion Retiro to San Isidro that morning by train, he gave me a thin, guileful smile and asked what I thought about the *villas* that had recently sprung up along the tracks. He was referring to the same shantytown that Sr. Campora had railed about two weeks before.

I didn't know what to say at first. Although I didn't admit it, I still believed the people living in those conditions had no alternative. I recently read in the local newspaper that the municipal government wanted to move them to the provinces, away from the capital. But there were no jobs in the provinces, no social programs, no services. So, I just shrugged and said there were no easy answers to the problem.

"Actually," he said, "there's a very simple answer. Drive them back to wherever they came from."

"Home to where?" I asked. "The provinces?"

"No, no! To Bolivia, Paraguay—that's where most of them are from anyway. Any place but in *our* city, our country," he said dismissively.

An uncomfortable silence settled in and took hold. I wanted to get away but had no polite excuse. So, instead, I conceded the point. "I suppose you are right, sir,"

Sr. Benitez shook his head and chuckled with a strange edge that bothered me.

"You suppose? Is it Paul?"

"Yes, my name is Paul."

"Paul, what?"

"Paul Casales."

"Well, Mr. Casales, you don't sound sure." The challenge was not subtle.

I was sure Sr. Benitez was prodding me. But what could I do? Sr. Benitez was one of Sr. Campora's colleagues. I remained silent, hoping he would drop the subject and go away.

Sr. Benitez asked why the poor concerned me. But again, I didn't have a ready answer. A ready and affirmative answer is what was expected. All I could think of saying was that it didn't seem right to berate them for their impoverishment. But I thought better of it. Sr. Benitez reached into his pocket and brought a carefully laundered handkerchief across his mouth. "Poverty has no place in our new Argentina," he stated, his voice agitated, bordering on anger.

Another moment of silence took hold. I bit my lower lip and smiled dutifully. Sr. Benitez emptied his cocktail.

"You do understand that, Mr. Casales?" His voice was firm, and there was no small smile.

"Yes, sir," I replied at last but warily.

"You can disagree with me if you wish," he stated.

"I don't disagree, sir."

"I think you do. Speak your mind!" he insisted.

"I just don't see why they should be treated like criminals," I offered, "just for being poor, sir."

"They *are* criminals—criminals and drug dealers. The *villas* are loaded with them. They are a blight!" His eyes bore into mine, and he gave me a pitying look and walked away. Clearly, I had not met the challenge. I sort of pitied him as well.

*

On this visit, Santiago showed me to a guest room adjacent to his own. I was disappointed that I would not be sleeping in Marco's room, but I did not read anything into it. We had all been up until the early hours of the morning and were exhausted. I awoke, drowsy and confused, to the sounds of Marco getting ready in his room. I didn't want to see anyone right then, so I rolled over and tried to doze again. When I woke the second time, I realized I was missing breakfast.

The intervening hour gave me time to myself to think about all that was happening to me. I had never been around people like those I met at the party. Their handshakes were firm, their speech measured but self-assured. Introductions were almost superfluous. It didn't matter whether they were from banking, oil, finance or chemicals or how much real power they had; it was well understood by everybody that together, they comprised something of a ruling class.

I thought about my mother. She would have resented these people almost as much as she resented military officers and their wives. It would have been just like her to assail their privileges and light into what she would have referred to as their self-gratification, their equanimity. I didn't feel that way. Yes, the guests at the party intimidated me, but as was the case with Agustin, I admired the way they were certain of their place in the world, the way they held their drinks and otherwise held themselves. I wanted to be like them, to be one of them. I realized then how important Sr. Campora was. He had influence and power. He could change things for me.

*

"I am sorry I am late," I said as I took a seat. It was eight in the morning, and the Camporas were already sitting at a round table in the kitchen. The room felt warm and safe. It was tidy and larger than any kitchen I had ever seen. Sr. Campora was taking Santiago through a list of guests, identifying who had talked with whom and what they spoke about. Marco and Juan were talking separately, laughing at something.

Sra. Campora was the first to speak to me. "Tell me what mischief you got up to last night. Did Marco keep his eyes on you?"

Marco answered for me. "Yes, Mother. And yes, Paul did very well, considering it was his first dive into the world of Campora garden parties," he said, trying to keep the tone light.

An inward sense of victory turned into a hopeful smile. Something important had happened to me. My future seemed brighter than it had been just twenty-four hours ago. It held more promise than ever before. Why? I think it was because I realized I was breaking out of my self-imposed shell. I was not destined to spend my life living my mother's life in a dreary apartment without friends or outside interests. At that moment, I was more at ease with myself than I had ever been.

I had packed my things and was with Marco in his room while he readied himself for our return to the capital on the two-thirty train. It was only eleven in the morning; we still had plenty of time to lark about and were joking about some of our experiences from the night before. Santiago abruptly knocked on the door.

"What are you up to in there?" he asked through the closed door.

"Nothing," Marco called back. "We're not ready yet."

"Then open the door," Santiago called back. "Father wants to speak with Paul." Marco looked at me from across the room and shrugged.

He opened the door and, in an audible whisper, asked Santiago, "What about."

Santiago said he didn't know. "Father just wants to see Paul alone in his library as soon as you finish packing."

I knocked on the library door. I was nervous. Had my awakening confidence been false? I could feel my heartbeat. Sr. Campora greeted me amicably, almost as though I was an old family friend. He acknowledged our train at two-thirty and got right to the point.

"Did you enjoy the party?"

I said yes and thanked him again for the invitation. I could not think of anything else to say.

"Marco thinks very highly of you and would like to see you more." I smiled but said nothing.

"Tell me about your mother," the interrogating intonation returned.

"My mother?"

"Yes. I believe you said you live alone with her. Is that right?"

"Yes, sir."

"Do you have other family? Perhaps there are cousins, for example?"

"Yes, sir. I believe I have two cousins in Rosario."

"You are not close to them?"

"Not really. My mother doesn't like to travel." I was on edge again.

"Are they on your father's side or your mother's?"

"My mother's. Her sister's children."

"So, she is not close to her sister?"

"Not really. I mean, they speak on the telephone sometimes, but we don't see her."

"And what about your uncle? What does he do?"

"I am not really sure, sir. Odd jobs mainly, I suppose."

As if he read my mind, Sr. Campora asked if he was poor.

"Sort of, sir. They are not impoverished, but they are poor."

"Do they live on social services?"

"Maybe, I suppose. I really don't know them well."

"I believe you mentioned to Sr. Benitez last night that people cannot help being poor. Were you thinking about your uncle?" he asked as directly as a prosecutor.

For a moment, I was stunned. I couldn't think of anything to say. Sr. Campora took a seat and looked at me from across his desk, waiting for my response. I still couldn't think of anything to say. My mind was racing. I wanted to rub my temples.

Finally, Sr. Campora leaned forward and spoke. The tone of his voice was still amicable, but his brow had tightened up.

"Paul," he said. "You seem to be a good boy, so I am going to talk candidly. I want you to listen carefully."

"Yes, sir," I said, trying hard to look right at him and not fidget.

"Argentina is changing." He talked for almost five or more minutes after that. It was a blur. He told me how subversives and radicals of varying kinds were terrorizing the cities and how the administration of Isabelita Perón was ineffective in dealing with the security situation. That's why the military *had* to seize the government. He said Sr. Benitez was right. The terrorists and criminals live among us, and the *villas* breed them.

When Sr. Campora was done, he reminded me of our first conversation at their country club and how I had spurned the idea of military service. He spoke of my beginnings, which he referred to as modest. He suggested that I should reconsider because a young man like me needs a good start, and the military would give me that.

"It's not that I dislike the military," I lied. "But my mother. She thinks the military depersonalizes men. She wants me to go to university and learn to think and speak for myself."

"With respect to your mother, that is a position that is terribly misinformed."

"What do you mean, sir?" I asked, almost hoping not to hear his answer.

"This notion of 'thinking and speaking for oneself' can lead to... unintended consequences." His voice was grave.

"I am not sure I understand, sir."

"Did you listen carefully to Admiral Massera's last speech? Do you recall him saying that some must speak and some must be still?"

"Yes, sir."

"These young people foolishly involved in the student movement don't understand this. Students are too young for politics. They don't have enough formal education or life experience to impose their ideas on society."

"Groups," he continued, "are infiltrated by subversives seeking to influence vulnerable children, especially student groups. *They* depersonalize men, *not* the military. You see how your mother is misinformed?"

I said I understood, but the truth is I think I still agreed with my mother. I felt that Sr. Campora had trapped me into saying otherwise.

"We are fighting for our very way of life, what it means to be Argentine and our ability to live in freedom."

That is why, he explained, there was a curfew in the capital. "The military needs to use every tool available to defeat the terrorists, including, in extreme cases, the same dirty tactics the terrorists themselves favor."

With that, Sr. Campora looked at his watch and stood up.

"It was good to talk with you," he said graciously. He shook my hand at the door of the study.

*

I only saw Marco at the gym intermittently for weeks after the party. He told me he wasn't feeling well and had exams coming up, and his father wanted him to commute more from home. Exams were scheduled to start in early May and continue for the better part of two weeks. For the time being, there wasn't much time for anything else or for me. I was lonely and a bit jealous, but mostly, I just wanted to get through this period and return to our routine.

When our exams were finally over, and we both returned to something of a routine, I was sitting quietly in the gym café with Agustin while around us, others stretched, lifted weights, ran, biked and rowed, all pretty much as normal. The windows were open, and we could sense the hints of autumn, which stirred my memory of the Campora's summer party just months before. As if he had read my mind, Agustin asked if everything was all right with Marco and with me. I was about to say *sure* when I realized the room had become mysteriously quiet.

Agustin also sensed the change. As he turned to take in the room, his face—which until then had been blank—looked strange.

The men closest to the walls were stirring like spooked animals caught between confusion and panic. Soon, they were moving back, away from the windows. There were quiet gasps and whispers, none of them discernible to me. Apprehension hung in the air like a storm cloud. Neither Agustin nor I knew what to think.

The word passed within moments. Two Falcons, first one and then another, had stopped at the curb in front of the gym. Two men in uniform were stopping traffic. Three more in civilian clothes were standing in the middle of the street, looking up at the gym from behind dark glasses.

Like the captain of a heaving ship, Agustin was neither calm nor frightened. Those around us were all in a daze. Some were murmuring, but each seemed to be hurriedly going over his own past, trying to recall what careless words or actions could have gotten him on the generals' lists and were preparing to explain how there must be some mistake. My mind slowly grasped what was, or might, be happening. My mind also was racing for recall.

Maya was right; I shouldn't have tried to make it home.

Sr. Benitez was right; poverty has no place in the new Argentina.

Sr. Campora was right; Argentina is changing.

I should never have mentioned foreign newspapers.

My mother...

Heavy footfalls on the old stairs interrupted my chaotic thoughts. I passed a quick glance over the room to Agustin. A group of men were seeking refuge in the locker room. Otherwise, no one was moving. Everything was silent when the men from the cars reached the top of the stairs. There were three of them now. Two, both dressed in military fatigues and hiding behind dark glasses, stepped into the café. The other stayed back, barely visible in the dark stairwell. From the little I could tell, he was dressed in some kind of black military garb, hooded and armed with a long rifle.

One of the two frontmen was the first to speak. In a deep voice with military crispness, he asked who was in charge. Agustin wavered at first, then stood. The man signaled his comrades to stay put and slowly, ever so slowly, proceeded toward him, glancing in step from side to side. As the man approached Agustin, he brushed my side and looked directly into my eyes. I thought I saw a flicker of recognition, and it was then, sensing the danger, that my face and every muscle tensed with anticipation. *Por no mi,* I silently prayed.

Until that moment, the Process was an abstraction, an obscenity that had been happening to others, not to me. Now, it had a face. *Next, they were going to write down my name,* I thought, *and just like that, I would be on a list.*

The man pushed Agustin forward toward the café. He put two pictures on the counter and asked if he knew them, one by one.

"Do you know this man?" Agustin shook his head no.

Then, bearing down, he asked if he knew the other. "What about this one?"

The man insisted that the men in the pictures worked out at the gym. But Agustin did not know either of them. Apparently satisfied he was telling the truth, the man backed off. He said they had no time to waste, and they would be watching. If either man was seen coming or going from the gym again, they would be back, and Agustin would regret their return.

When the men were gone, I took a shower and closed the door of my locker as though I was abandoning it forever. Things would be different with the gym from now on. My mother might forbid me to return. I could say there had been some kind of mistake, but she would not believe me. She would say the military was very deliberate and didn't make mistakes like that. They would return.

It was just after six o'clock. I said goodbye to a shaken Agustin and walked to the area of the movie theatres on Callao. I found a movie that was just starting, bought a ticket, and took a seat just as the trailers came on. When the film was over, I wished it would start again.

*

The film was about two young friends growing up in New York. Their ordinary lives were similar, and their smiles bright. Naturally, it made me think of Marco. I often dreamed of being life-long friends despite the many ways Marco and I were dissimilar. As my mother frequently cautioned, "Marco's family is rich. He will soon graduate from *Collegio Nacionale* and go on to a university full of other kids like him."

Dreams aside, I was realistic. I had college plans of my own, but they were relatively modest compared to his. In comparison, it had always been obvious that Marcos's future was somewhat pre-ordained—his father would have a big say in his choice of schools, careers and every other aspect of his future. At times, I thought Sr. Campora, and possibly Santiago too, were becoming concerned that I might be a bad influence on Marco. Neither of them ever said as much. But I often sensed it, like when Sr. Campora drilled me on my relationships with my own mother and father, what I thought he viewed as my indifference toward military service and some of my social views. Ironically, the truth was the other way around. Following Marco's example, I began seriously entertaining thoughts about college and beyond. Despite our limited resources, for the first time in my life, I was beginning to realize that I had options and pondered what they might be. I was determined to become someone worthy of other people's respect.

May 1978

On 23 May, Paul left his last class, returned some books to his locker and took out others that he would need to do his homework. As usual, he was running late and had to sprint to the corner of Avenida Cordoba to catch his bus, the #132. The autumn air was bright and dry, wind tugged at the yellowing leaves on the trees. Puffy clouds crossed the sky, and the sun came and went. Paul was full of happy expectations. Marco was meeting him at the café for the first time in weeks.

He made it just in time. The brightly colored bus arrived in a plume of diesel fuel, its brakes hissing air and its body squeaking and rattling. After many passengers piled out, Paul flashed his school pass and headed for a seat near the rear door. He had no patience for the bus's idling engine; he was anxious to see Marco and itching to get underway.

When the bus finally pulled away from the curb, it suddenly jerked and stopped again, nearly throwing the standing passengers to the floor. As Paul turned to apologize for stomping on the foot of a man standing in front of him, a tall soldier wearing a black face mask and fatigues boarded through the front door. The driver sat motionless, face and eyes straight ahead, nervously waiting for instructions. Some of the passengers could not see the soldier at first, but everyone sensed his presence. The soldier slowly made his way down the aisle, stopping every few steps to look closely at passengers on his right and left. Each, in turn, averted the soldier's eyes and otherwise tried to make himself invisible, breathlessly waiting for him to move on and exhaling deeply when he did.

The area around the back door was choked with the passengers. The soldier ordered them to clear a path, but there was nowhere to go. When they didn't move quickly enough, he got agitated and started pushing people out of his way rudely at first, then roughly, eventually brandishing his pistol in one hand and elbowing through the crowd with the other. *Don't look at anything, just look down.* Following his mother's advice, Paul's head turned down and away as the soldier approached. Soon, he was looking directly at the soldier's black leather boots and, like everyone before him, breathlessly waiting for him to move away.

The events that followed were only partly visible to Paul. The soldier signaled something to other soldiers standing outside, one of whom immediately boarded the bus through the back door, stopping just long enough at the top of the stairs to check his mask. *Keep looking down.* Out of the corner of an eye, Paul saw the second soldier approaching and then a third. *Whatever happens, don't look up.* Paul repeated this to himself like a mantra.

Before he knew what was happening, the soldier standing directly over him took hold of Paul's arm and ordered him to get up. The events that followed were quick and well-practiced. One soldier sat calmly in the front seat of the Falcon, idling alongside the bus, occasionally drawing on a cigarette. Two others cleared the aisle, and the fourth, pistol in hand, backed Paul toward the door. When they reached it, he wrapped his arm around Paul's neck.

"*Por mi cuello, no*, not by the neck," Paul pleaded.

Paul knew the other passengers felt no pity for him. They were just relieved and wanted the bus to get underway. Nevertheless, he screamed his name, "I am Paul Casales, 605 Esmeral…!" A heavy boot buried itself in his groin, and then everything went white, and his knees buckled. The soldiers pushed him to the ground, face down. Asphalt, pebbles and dirt filled his entire field of vision. Moments later, the bus pulled away, its engine straining and belching, its rear wheel passing so close that Paul feared the soldiers might push his head under it. Instead, as the bus merged into the steady flow of traffic, a cloud of sooty diesel exhaust in its wake, the soldiers pulled him to his feet and stuffed him into the back seat of the Falcon.

As the #132 gained speed and proceeded along its route, the driver put the Falcon in gear and pulled away. It was headed to the *Escuela de Mecánica de Armada*, the now infamous 'Navy School of Mechanics', (usually just ESMA), the largest detention center of its kind during the 'Dirty War' and the seat of Task Force 3.3.2, a clandestine and brutal military brigade. It was around four-thirty when the Falcon arrived. Paul tried to focus his thoughts on the café where, he figured, Marco was still waiting. *He will wonder where I am.* When he looked out the window, he was surprised to see red and white neoclassical administration buildings and manicured lawns, and probably took some comfort from the fact that the ESMA looked more like a university than a secret detention center. But the Falcon passed by all three of the ornate rod iron gates on Avenida Libertador and drove, instead, to one of the plain iron gates along Calle Leopoldo Lugones. Paul took note of the changed appearance of the compound. Instead of the freshly painted colonnaded buildings, scrolled gates and neat lawns along Libertador, this side was bordered by a high stone wall over which he could see rows of drab military barracks.

After it was cleared by the uniformed guards at the gate, the Falcon proceeded slowly toward the rear of one of the buildings. Soldiers ambling about the compound squinted to look through its windows as it pulled up to a heavy metal door and came to a stop. Moments later, they plucked Paul from the back seat and shoved him into the arms of even more soldiers just inside the doorway. On their orders, he trudged down a long hallway and into a windowless room where, as instructed, he sat on one of four bare metal chairs, the room's only furnishings. The room was cold and damp and smelled of disinfectant. The cement floor and walls were both dirty, and there was blaring music coming from somewhere else deep inside the building. He heard something that sounded like screaming but couldn't be sure. It was as if someone was talking in an adjoining room.

Barely an hour had passed since the soldiers took Paul off the bus, but to him, sitting there under those circumstances, it seemed like an eternity. He took some comfort from the fact that just a single young soldier was guarding him now, and he wasn't handcuffed. But his efforts to remain calm were dashed. The soldiers soon returned, and within minutes, he was crying and shaking violently. He couldn't conceal his terror.

One of the soldiers, impressed by Paul's distress, said that he was taking over and dismissed the guard. "Stand up," he commanded, followed immediately by "strip." As he did as he was told, his mind drifted beyond the walls around him. *Mother will be waiting for me at home in her chair reading. Marco will be at the gym by now.* Then, the worst thought of all passed in front of him. *Perhaps they have Marco, too.*

When Paul finished undressing, the soldier put a hood over his head and backed him into a corner. By then, Paul was practically hyperventilating. More soldiers came into the room, and the beatings began. They beat him with rubber hoses easily at first, as if they were trying to soften him up, and then harder. The beatings continued randomly, almost as if recreationally for the guards, for more than a week. Paul remained hooded and naked in a small, filthy cell the entire time. The only time the doors opened was to admit more soldiers with hoses. The beatings came frequently and got worse. One evening, the door opened, and three soldiers entered, each ducking his head to clear the low ceiling. Paul instinctively drew back into a corner as if to disappear, to shield himself from the blows and insults that he knew were coming. Oddly, there were no blows. This time, he felt instead a warm sensation that, at first, he couldn't identify. Without so much as a word, all three soldiers, each in turn, urinated on him. All the while, they joked and babbled about something. Paul could barely make out the words. He thought they were saying fish food.

Part Two

The Noise of Broken Chains

Buenos Aires, 1983

Now twenty-three, Marco seldom questioned and never regretted his decision to pursue a career in journalism. He was sure it was the most important personal decision he had made in his still young life. The decision cost him dearly in terms of his father's support. Señor Campora had always assumed his three sons would serve in the military and pursue military careers. Despite some misgivings arising from the generals' handling of the Process, he continued to hold military officers in high esteem. To many Argentines, and certainly to Sr. Campora, a military career still was seen as a sure path to a life of privilege, power and prestige. In contrast, journalists were seen by many in society, including Sr. Campora, as leftists or democratic socialists disguised as reporters but really anarchists in one form or another. Marco had thought hard to come to a different view. To his mind, true journalists spent a lifetime developing skills with which to pursue truth toward noble ends.

*

Marco keenly focused on the importance of the interview he was going to. If he got the internship, it would be an important first step in pursuit of his career. Although he missed the last bus, there was plenty of time. It was just half past noon, and the interview was not until two o'clock. He took a seat on a wide curbside bench to wait for the next bus. It was a warm and sunny afternoon. He was preoccupied with his own business, barely paying any attention to the cacophony of chatter and laughter coming from the men in suits all around him who were lunching or hurrying to meetings. He sensed someone approaching. A middle-aged woman asked if she could share the bench. Without looking up, he hurriedly removed his briefcase and papers from his side to clear a space for her. "Of course, please," he said and gestured for her to sit.

"Thank you."

"You're welcome," Marco answered a bit absently.

"Perhaps you are late to be in your office?" the woman observed, with Marco fidgeting with his briefcase and eyeing down the street for an approaching bus.

Marco let out a nervous breath. "I don't have an office. I don't even have a job." He then began a disorganized ramble: he was seeking an internship with *This Week;* he wanted to cover the national news; he was a recent graduate of the university; he was on his way right then for a hard-to-get interview; yes, he was nervous!

"Whoa!" the woman chuckled. "You have a big afternoon ahead of you. Take a long breath."

"I'll tell you what," she quickly added, "I am on my way to a meeting close to *This Week's* offices. Let me treat us both to a taxi."

Marco was about to decline the offer when the woman said, "C'mon. We can talk a bit; take your mind off the interview."

Marco quickly started gathering his papers and stuffing them into his briefcase.

"Slow down," the woman said. "You've got plenty of time."

By now, some ten minutes had passed since this stranger had taken her seat on their shared bench. Marco finally glanced at her. Her dark hair was perfectly coifed, and she was conservatively dressed in a navy blue two-piece pantsuit. Marco imagined that she was a businesswoman. Neither Marco nor the woman spoke as they crossed the street toward the taxi line.

"My name is Christina," the woman smiled and said. "I am supposing you have a name too?"

It had not occurred to Marco, whose training in manners was ingrained, to introduce himself.

"Oh! I am sorry. I am Marco."

"I am pleased to meet you, Marco."

He apologized a second time and quickly added, "My full name is Marco Campora; it is my pleasure to meet you as well."

"Ah, you have redeemed yourself with a first *and* last name," she said with a smile. "Your mother might have been ashamed of your manners this afternoon."

You don't know the half of it, Marco thought. Again, he found himself momentarily at a loss for conversation.

Christina broke the silence as soon as she settled next to Marco in the taxi. "Well, you aim high. *This Week* is widely regarded as one of the finest English-language periodicals in the Americas. If you are going to get this job and be successful at it, you are going to have to find your voice."

For most of the rest of the ride, she explained how *This Week* was known for breaking with the traditional national emphasis on propaganda to stress professional, accurate news reporting. Then she hit on what really got Marco excited at the prospect of working there: *This Week's* commitment to human rights or, as she put it, "Its continuing concern for human welfare."

Marco was about to ask his new acquaintance a brazen question of how she knew so much about where he was going just as the taxi was fast approaching its stop. A bus in front of the taxi stopped to discharge passengers, giving Marco just enough time to ask Christina if or how she might be affiliated with *This Week*.

"My work often brings me there," she replied. Before Marco could ask why, the taxi stopped in front of *This Week's* office building, and they got out. He only briefly recaptured Christina's attention after she paid the taxi fare, for which Marco politely thanked her. He wanted to know more about his new acquaintance. Rather than a proper farewell, however, Christina's relaxed smile seemed to say, "Oh well, I am sorry we don't have more time."

Christina said a brisk goodbye on the sidewalk. There was nothing more—no 'good luck' or 'I hope to see you again' or 'Do you have a business card?' When Marco said goodbye, she had already turned. Not sure whether he would ever see the woman again, he watched as she merged quickly with the foot traffic. She had popped in and out of his life in less than an hour, or so he thought.

*

Nattily dressed businessmen were passing through the massive lobby at a brisk pace—all business-like, few smiles, fewer greetings—mostly just a seemingly laser-like focus on their business there. Marco shot a quick glance toward a man standing by himself off to the side. He imagined this man, slightly disheveled and frumpish, had to be a beat reporter; he certainly looked the part. The man genially returned the glance.

"Excuse me," said Marco as he approached him. "I am looking for Room 901. I haven't seen a building directory, and I have an appointment there in twenty minutes, a job interview, actually."

The man pointed to the middle elevator bank and began to explain to Marco where to go when he arrived on the ninth floor. Apparently, thinking he could be more helpful if he knew with whom Marco had an appointment, he asked.

"I actually don't know," said Marco, "I was told to go to Room 901 and ask for Long; just Long."

The man chuckled. "Good ol' Esteban Long. He's been around here forever."

"Oh, you know him?" Marco asked.

"Not really," he answered. "Let's just say I do things for him and others from time to time. The newspaper business has been in my blood for as long as I can remember, down here in Argentina and up in Boston, where I am from."

Marco introduced himself, and they shook hands. The man introduced himself as Ash Collins, an ex-pat. Marco thought that he had been right. This dowdy man epitomized Marco's stereotype of an old-time reporter who had been around. He was wondering what kind of things he did for Long when Collins gestured toward Room 901, which was not exactly a 'room'. It was a busy, brightly lit, but smoke-hazed newsroom with numerous fans hung from the ceiling over rows of gray metal desks.

Collins peered into the room and waved to a stern woman standing just inside the doorway. As she made her way toward them, Collins told Marco that she was Long's executive assistant. Marco recognized the name Marguerite Manning as the woman he had previously spoken with on the telephone.

When Manning reached them, Collins immediately took charge of the situation. Nudging Marco forward, he said in a jovial voice, "This is the guy you are waiting for: *This Week's* next hot-shot reporter! Introduce yourself, kid."

Standing stiffly and slightly embarrassed, Marco nodded, introduced himself and offered his hand. Marco pointed to his briefcase and said he had brought several writing samples. "Hold on to them," she said flatly, "Señor Long may wish to see them later."

Manning turned away, dismissively thanked Collins for his assistance, and asked Marco to follow her. After adding his own thanks, he did. On their way to the head of the cavernous newsroom, Manning asked Marco how he knew Christina Darin.

It took Marco a moment to register who she was talking about.

"Christina Darin?" he repeated.

Manning paused in her steps, turned and explained that Darin was the woman with whom Marco had just shared a taxi. Quickly, Marco surmised that his new acquaintance had even more knowledge about *This Week* than he had imagined. She had speculated that Marco probably would be interviewing with Long and had the clout to call Manning to put in a good word for him.

Marco had a well-rehearsed idea of what he was going to say to Long when he got the chance. He never did, at least not that afternoon. Shortly after three o'clock had come and gone, Marco stole a quick look at his watch. Not wanting to appear irritated or impatient, he resisted the temptation to glance at it too often. He was sure it was close to four o'clock, an hour later when Manning informed him that Long was being called away unexpectedly to an urgent editorial meeting on the twelfth floor. Confused, Marco didn't know if that was 'it' or if the interview would be rescheduled. Manning asked Marco to stay seated for just a little while longer as Long wanted at least to greet him on his way upstairs.

As Marco waited, three men hurried past him and silently disappeared into Long's office. A few minutes later, they reemerged with Long and Manning. At first, it did not look like they were going to stop; their shoes beat at a quick pace across the wooden floor. As they approached, however, Long stopped, gave Marco a wary look, apologized for the change of plans, and extended his right hand. Despite being short and heavy, Long's appearance was just as Marco had imagined: he looked old (but perhaps was younger than he looked) with long bushy eyebrows, thinning gray hair and penetrating dark eyes. He definitely looked the part. He held his suit jacket over his left shoulder, and a wrinkled white shirt, which may have started the day pressed and neatly tucked into his trousers, was rolled up at the sleeve, and one of his shirttails was loose. Like the warrior Marco imagined him to be, he had an unwrapped cigar in the shirt pocket together with several pens in a worn-out vinyl pocket protector.

"I just got off the telephone with Ms. Darin," Long said. "The call was quite unusual for her. You made a very favorable impression." Taken aback, Marco shook his hand, and as he scrambled to think of a response, Long said, "Welcome to my staff, Mr. Campora." Marco wasn't sure he heard that right until Long added that if

Marco would allow *This Week* to impose upon his time for just a little while longer, Ms. Manning would gather the forms he would need to fill out.

"The job is an internship. You may consider yourself a junior assistant with some writing duties." At that, Long's mind seemed to switch back to more mundane things. "You will start on Monday morning. Please bring the papers back at that time." Long gave Manning a few final instructions and gave Marco a quick welcome-to-the-team pat on the right shoulder before continuing at a hurried pace with the two silent men flanking his sides.

When Long was safely out of earshot, Manning revealed that Darin had called Long and done more than put in a 'good word' for Marco. She had endorsed him wholeheartedly as 'just the kind of 'new blood' you could use more of over there'. Long respected Darin, who apparently also said she might hire Marco if he did not.

A few minutes later, Marco was back in the building's massive lobby. He closed his eyes and proudly imagined himself a part of *This Week*, validation of his decision to become a journalist in the first place. He wouldn't dwell on that for now; his mind was on other things. He could now support himself and call home to San Isidro with good news for him that he hoped would be greeted as good news by them.

*

The Thomson Reuters headquarters on Calle Tucaman was as impressive in its own way as *This Week's*.

Surrounded by multiple television monitors silently broadcasting live news headlines from various world capitals, Marco felt the full weightiness of the company's global reach and influence. A week before, Marco found himself reverently standing in *This Week's* impressive lobby. Now, a week later, he stood for another moment, again awed by the tools used by news and other professionals to provide the world with essential information.

In response to Marco's questions over the past week, Manning eventually revealed to Marco that Darin did, indeed, work for Reuters. She explained that she was an executive in its corporate foundation. According to Manning, the Foundation was well known for its dedication to advancing human rights in Argentina and internationally, and Darin was regarded as one of the Foundation's most highly recognized and influential assets, perhaps the most.

Marco used the building directory in the lobby to find that the offices of the Foundation were on the third floor. When Marco appeared in the reception area, the receptionist was rushing to finish a draft letter to the United Nations Office on Drugs and Crime regarding human trafficking.

"Good afternoon," Marco said. "May I leave this note for Ms. Darin?"

"*Mrs.* Darin is not in the building. I believe she will be traveling for the rest of the week," she said with a tone of finality.

"Will she receive it if I leave it with you?" Marco asked.

"May I ask what your business is?"

Marco explained how the two of them had met the week before and how Darin was so gracious and instrumental in him becoming a newly hired intern at *This Week*. The note was a thank you.

"Please leave it with me," she said. "I will put it on her desk and be sure she sees it as soon as she returns. Will Mrs. Darin know where to reach you? Do you have a business card?"

Slightly embarrassed, Marco said he did not have one yet. She suggested he write it down on a blank card she was handing to him. Marco did as the receptionist suggested and scribbled another *Thank you!* On the back.

Something about Marco's nervous demeanor made the receptionist wonder if Marco was a smitten young suitor or an ambitious young over-achiever just seeking to improve his position. She held these thoughts as she swiveled back into position in front of her big Underwood typewriter. *God help him if it's the former*, she thought.

*

Marco was tasked at first with routine assignments, proofreading mostly. He was eager to move up from a proofreader to editing, where he could use some of the writing skills for which he won several awards at university. However, he was determined to bring a high level of commitment to even the most mundane tasks. He was working on such a task when Manning called him to the office just outside Long's.

"I was asked to hand this to you," she said. She handed Marco a sealed envelope and then turned to answer one of two telephone calls that beckoned her.

The letter was neatly handwritten on personal stationery and signed *Christina Darin*. The way she wrote the letter 't' tipped Marco to the fact that Christina had either attended Catholic school or been home-schooled by the nuns. *Thank you for your thoughtful visit. I enjoyed meeting you, and I am sorry the taxi ride was so short. I will be pleased if you will have lunch with me. Please let me know.* There was a telephone number at the top of the page.

Marco wanted to call immediately, but he decided to wait until he got home that evening. Long's strict policy was no personal telephone calls from the office or use of a company telephone for personal purposes. Also, Marco did not know what to expect when he rang the number that Christina had given him, her private number. He felt as though he had just been promoted, or got a raise, or received good news from home. He was both excited and nervous about the prospect of speaking with Christina again.

Marco dialed the telephone as soon as he got home. Christina picked up on the second ring. He tried to picture her on the other end of the line: what she looked like and what she was doing. He imagined her in a silk robe, sitting at a desk at home, going through business papers with a television monitor on silently in the background.

Marco wondered how many other people Christina had selected for the attention she was giving him. Also, he wondered if what she was doing was calculated to achieve some end that was just part of her work. Maybe she really did believe he was destined to become a good journalist. Or was he being used in some way to her benefit? To Marco, it did not matter. He just hoped that maybe there would be some room in the acquaintance for friendship, times when she would digress from her agenda and possibly even let herself go off script altogether. The important thing to bear in mind, he reminded himself, is she is someone who could have a significant influence on his career.

"So, how is the job going?" Christina asked Marco, right to the point.

"Thanks in no small part to you; I could not be more thrilled," he said. "Really, thank you again for your help and for this chance." Marco heard himself say a bit too excitedly.

"I would like to take you to lunch on Saturday," Christina responded—all business.

"That would be very generous of you," Marco said. "I am mostly free on the weekends."

Marco could hear her thinking out loud as she rustled through the pages of her appointment calendar.

"Three o'clock? Let's meet in the lobby of the Savoy. It should be quiet at that hour, and we can talk."

"I look forward to it."

*

Although he was not generally an early riser, Marco woke and got up unusually early on Saturday morning. He had no laundered shirts left in his closet, necessitating a trip to the laundromat as soon as it opened. On the way, he thought he would stop and have his shoes shined. He expected Christina to be turned out smartly as usual, and he wanted to look his best.

The afternoon was warm and sunny. All of Buenos Aires seemed to be in the streets and especially alive. He and Christina both arrived promptly at three. She wore a very smart mustard-colored dress with a red jacket and matching headband. While the hostess fumbled for two menus and the wine list, Christina spoke to Marco in a way that made him feel like a friend rather than a business colleague of sorts.

When they were comfortably seated, the waiter asked Christina if she wanted the 'usual'. She said no and then ordered for both of them. "My young friend and I are celebrating this afternoon, so let's have something special." With that, she handed the wine list back to the waiter and directed him to choose.

As soon as the waiter turned and walked away, Christina unfolded her napkin and said, "You have already made a favorable impression on Long. I'm pleased for you." She offered a wry smile.

Marco smiled in return but said nothing in reply. He wondered what he should say. Thankfully, Christina did not wait for his answer and went right on talking and inquiring about Marco's background. Christina listened intently to Marco as if every detail was of interest. Marco found it easy not to hold back. He recounted how he had once revered his father, how his brothers had been his best friends growing up, and how he was no longer as close to them as he used to be, especially his older brother. They went on talking about personal things for more than a half hour. Christina took a pause, leaned in closer to Marco and changed the subject, asking in a lower voice, "Was life difficult for you during the military's rule? Did it affect you?"

"Of course, it affected me," Marco responded. "Students like me were affected disproportionately. Targeted, really." Marco quickly clarified that he was referring to students in general and not to himself. He added that the randomness of the military actions and the mystery of it all were still confusing and troubling.

"You must have a lot of questions," she said, "There are many people looking for answers." Her gaze was intent, but at that point, Christina stopped talking, and neither of them said anything more on the subject.

When the momentary silence was broken, Christina offered Marco her right hand and said, "This has been a nice opportunity to get to know you better." When she stood up, Marco wondered why he had revealed so much about himself and felt slightly, somehow manipulated. He was concerned that she may have had some reason for getting him to talk so much. As he wondered what that might be, they said goodbye in the lobby and promised to see each other again. But, he wondered, why?

*

After two months on the job, Marco had come to expect being called into the office on weekends. The current news cycle was dominated by raised expectations for the return of a democratic government and some freedoms. That prospect and the election had displaced yesterday's headlines: the continuing fallout over the loss of the *Las Malvinas*, intermittent wage freezes, policies adverse to industry, restrictive measures like Circular 1050, and anemic GDP per capita.

On Saturday morning, Long was not in his office. No one was. It was only Marco, another intern and Manning. Marco didn't think that mattered much. Everyone understood that Manning pretty much ran the newsroom, and she was there behind her desk, as usual, without fail. Upon his arrival, she gave Marco some readers' correspondence to answer, but nothing urgent. It occurred to Marco that morning that he had not written anything of any real importance since Long offered him the internship and told him his title would be a junior assistant *'with some writing duties'*. He looked forward to a time when the writing duties part would become a reality.

Marco did not have to wait long; it was just after noon. Marco fought the temptation to step out for lunch. Instead, he picked up another reader's letter, this one concerning conditions in Argentina's wine industry. Marco was in the process of composing his response when Manning interrupted him to say Long would be coming into the office after all, and he had a writing assignment for him. Long was expected to arrive within the hour and in the meantime, she instructed, he wanted Marco to 'bone up' on the short presidency of Reynaldo Bignone.

Marco vaguely remembered some things about Bignone's administration but the details were few. Bignone's term in office was two years ago. At that time, Marco was finishing his studies at the university. However, the impression Marco did have was that it was not a particularly eventful presidency.

Long stood in front of Marco's desk, the usual cigarette in hand. Pointing to the narrow reporter's notebook in front of Marco, Long told Marco to take notes. Marco was more than ready. Without hesitation, Long started in. "Since this is your first writing assignment, I will take it slow. Ready?" He asked, not expecting or waiting for an affirmative response. "Here's your summary."

"Bignone's installation as president was hotly opposed in some military quarters. You may refer to him in this assignment as Argentina's last dictator." He went on to explain that Bignone will be remembered for two things: allowing political parties to resume activities and announcing general elections. The other members of the junta, especially Admiral Massera, feared that Bignone's policies would lead to a democratically elected president sympathetic to society's growing demands for justice. Long took a drag on his cigarette and paused at this moment to emphasize his point.

"Here's the crux of the assignment. The generals' big fear was if they agreed to hold elections and transfer power to a civilian government, the new president, whomever that might be, would call for the generals to be put on trial for war crimes—make those crimes against humanity. Devoting themselves to damage control, the regime is suspected of preparing for the transition by shredding evidence.

"Do you see where this is going? Somewhere, probably in the vast underground of the generals' headquarters, there are miles of metal shelving. And there, secret and not to be opened until way in the future or written in some way that only a few could encode, are files on the 'disappeared,' perhaps all of them. The files' destruction would be a crime second only to the heinous kidnappings themselves." Long was on a roll.

After a deep breath and a long pause, during which Long took another drag on his cigarette and appeared to be asking himself if he left out anything, he finally said, "There you have it, the start and the finish."

"Your assignment," he said, "is to give me fifteen hundred words, two thousand max, on how the files must be preserved. Otherwise, the victims' loved ones would be left to forever wonder what happened. Even worse, it will make it much more difficult to hold the generals responsible for their actions and, thus, deprive the nation of a means of healing and coming back together. Oh, and write it up as a speech."

With a skeptical smile, Long finished, "Don't let me down, Campora. I have to present this at an awards dinner next week." That was only the second time Long had referred to Marco by name.

*

"Speaking of awards," Long asked, "have you heard that the Thomson Reuters Foundation is receiving the International Humanitarian Award for your friend's series on the living conditions in the Buenos Aires' slums—*las miserias*?"

"You mean Mrs. Darin? She is really just an acquaintance," Marco replied. "I have not heard from her for more than a month."

"Well, the Humanitarian Award is considered quite an honor. Darin won't tell you herself," Long added. "That's not her nature. You ought to reach out to congratulate her."

Marco was aware that Christina was keenly interested in housing equality issues, but he was not aware of her reporting on the subject. Thanks to a little research he did in *This Week's* microfiche library, Marco learned that her reporting about the conditions in *Barrio 31*, home to the poorest of the poor, made progress possible. It opened the door to obtain funding for a new project that had been providing free, high-quality medical care for over five years, demonstrably reducing the number of deaths among the Barrios' occupants.

*

A week later, Marco's doorbell rang very early on Sunday morning. He buzzed just in case it was someone from the office. When Marco opened his door, there was a man standing in front of him. The man was dressed in a dark suit and black cap, a uniform of sorts. He introduced himself as Mrs. Darin's driver.

"I was asked to deliver this to you," he said and handed Marco a small, light blue envelope.

The note inside was from Christina. Apparently, it referred to the congratulatory note Marco had posted to her. *Thank you for your very kind note. I hope you are free to have supper tonight with my husband and me. I will send a driver to bring you.* As before, the letter was signed 'Christina', and there was a telephone number for Marco to call.

Marco politely accepted the dinner invitation but declined her offer to send a driver. Rather, he decided to take a taxi to their Puerto Madero apartment. Marco chuckled as he stepped into the luxuriously appointed lobby, thinking that the taxi driver must have thought Marco was someone important.

As soon as Marco rang the bell, he could hear the sound of footsteps approaching the door. The door was opened by a uniformed valet. The valet led Marco to a drawing room. He announced that Christina and her husband would be in soon and asked if Marco would like something to drink.

"No," Marco replied. "I will wait for them."

Marco was admiring the view of the port outside the floor-to-ceiling windows when Christina and her husband appeared. When Marco turned around, Alberto Darin introduced himself and shook his hand. He was a bit shorter than Marco expected, with ample dark hair and a short, waxed mustache. On first impression, he appeared to be even more formal than Christina. For her part, Christina unexpectedly leaned in for a kiss and remarked on Marco's jacket and tie and how handsome he looked. Alberto was dressed in a rumpled linen suit and a bow tie, an interesting contrast to Christina's not-so-casual black evening dress and jewelry.

They sipped martinis. At first, Alberto did most of the talking. He went on about Omaha, Nebraska (he was an expat); Ronald Reagan (he was a social democrat); and curiously, Marco thought, about Reagan's choice for his ambassodor to the United Nations, Jeanne Kirkpatrick (he was a political junkie).

Marco sensed that Christina wanted to say something. He was curious what that might be when a server entered and announced that dinner was to be served and asked them to follow her to the dining room. A polished table was set for just the three of them. Christina pointed Alberto toward the head of the table and then directed Marco to sit on his right. She sat across on Alberto's left, making it easy to have a conversation.

While they were dining, Christina thanked Marco again for his note and sort of sermonized on the state of the economy and its effects on human rights. Marco had no idea where this was going. "To be sure," she said, "people are preoccupied with their own well-being as measured by their own job prospects, personal finances, the economy as a whole and inflation." Then she added, "It concerns me, however, that they may become callous without even realizing their callousness when it comes to social welfare programs and human rights."

Before Alberto or Marco could say anything on the topic, her expression changed. It became serious, and her tone businesslike. Even the server seemed to sense it; she instinctively turned back toward the kitchen and closed the door.

"That said," Christina went on, "my grave concern right now is the disappearances and senselessness of the generals' brutality and what we as a nation are going to do about that." Looking directly across at Marco, she forcefully said Argentina must never forget. "We need truth," she emphasized, a nod, Marco thought, to the proposals being floated in various social democratic circles for the establishment of a South African-like truth and reconciliation commission.

Clearly impatient to make his point, Alberto broke in. "In contrast to my dear wife, I go back and forth on whether to punish the perpetrators or to just let bygones be bygones," he started. Then he continued. "The idea of tribunals seems desirable on the surface, but it is risky. Tribunals may further alienate the country's traditional power players, the very people we need to bring the country back together—legitimate military rulers, the hierarchy of the Church and conservatives."

Christina cut him short, "There is no evidence of that. It is simply not the case."

Feeling confident, Marco agreed with Christina. "We have to address the responsibility of Argentine society while the state was committing mass atrocities." He then recited an excerpt from the speech he had written for Long at the Humanitarian Awards dinner: "A society that does not acknowledge its history does not properly heal—it cannot look forward by forgetting its past and will simply pretend to be at peace." He hoped Christina did not recognize it as a lifted passage. Whether his pronouncement was regarded as profound or naïve, it seemed to put a cap on the topic.

When dinner was made, and he was excused, Marco stepped out to see the 'driver' already had called a taxi and motioned for him to wait. As he did, Marco wondered whether he had offended his hosts and what they were saying to each other right at that moment.

*

The office was quiet, as it usually was on Monday morning. The day's news would not start coming in until around noon, at which time the newsroom would swing into rackety action, and that week's edition would begin to take shape. Marco was supposed to be finishing a column about the impact of the proposed tax reforms on capital formation that he had started editing on Saturday. But his mind was lingering on the prior evening's dinner with the Darins. He still worried that he said more than he should have about the responsibility of Argentine society, which, after all, the Darins had been part of. He regretted opening his mouth and echoing Long's words. The irony, he thought, was the words were not his own because, actually, Marco had yet to form a definitive opinion on the subject. He was fairly confident Christina agreed with what he said, but Alberto almost certainly found it impudent.

Marco's train of thought was interrupted by a telephone call. Long instructed him to take a break from the column he was working on and to come to his office. This was unusual. Long usually came to Marco's desk in the newsroom when he had something to say. On the rare occasions Marco was asked to see Long in his office, the request was relayed by Ms. Manning. He feared Christina might have recognized that Marco's words at dinner had been borrowed from Long's speech and reported that to Long.

Long was seated with his legs crossed on the edge of the desk, his face a silhouette in a haze of cigarette smoke. He motioned for Marco to be seated as he drew a long last whiff from his cigarette and snuffed it out before speaking. Sure enough, the conversation involved Christina Darin. But it was not the conversation Marco was expecting.

"Christina thinks you might turn out to be a special talent that I should take care to nurture." Then, chuckling, he said, "I don't think anyone considers me to be the nurturing type."

Only half-chuckling now, Long asked Marco if he thought he had what it takes to be a 'special talent'?

"I believe I eventually could be," Marco replied, a bit surprised by his own bravado.

Then, looking Marco straight in the eyes, Long asked several questions in rapid fire: what are your goals; are you committed to journalism; are you willing to commit to *This Week*?

Marco was not sure which question to answer first— or how. "I am still young in years and in experience. I am just realizing options and evaluating my potential."

Marco continued, "This is my first real-world job. That said, meeting Ms. Darin has made me think a lot about the future. She is a model for what I want to become. And working here, I discover opportunities every day to make a difference for good."

"And that is?" Long interrupted.

"I want to be successful, like her and you, of course. I know this phrase is over-used, but along the way, I want to contribute to positive change in our society and people's real lives."

"How so?"

Marco thought for a moment before answering. "For example, I would like to help in some small way to build our new democracy."

"That's quite an ambitious goal for a young man," Long said without sounding condescending.

"I understand," Marco replied. "This may sound naïve or simplistic, but I think the future of Argentina depends on every one of us working toward the same democratic goal—those who can in a big way, but everyone in small ways."

Long's response surprised Marco. "It *is* idealistic, maybe even a bit callow, but what's wrong with that?" He added that throughout history, including Argentina's recent history. "Youthful idealism has been a powerful force for change." After a short pause during which Long was apparently thinking, he confessed, "Perhaps this old man could use a fresh dose of it myself." Then he sat up straight and instructed Marco to listen up and take notes.

"You talk about opportunity? You did a good job on my speech at the awards dinner, so I have a new assignment." Long asked what Marco knew about the proposed *Full Stop Law*. "I am going to give you some background material, some of which may be familiar to you even though you were a student during most of the events I will be describing."

For Marco's benefit, Long started to describe how candidate Raul Alfonsín sought the presidency on a campaign of truth and justice. Alfonsín repeatedly stated that the illegal actions committed by the military must be adjudicated by Argentina's judicial system and not just by history, a big factor in his election. In anticipation of an Alfonsín election victory, the military commanders' last official act was to pass an amnesty law to ensure they would never be tried in civilian courts for human rights violations.

"Now, flash forward to when the democratic government was seated later that year," Long continued, "Alfonsín was true to his word." He explained that, after Alfonsín's inauguration, the new president promptly instituted a plan of military accountability. He recognized that he had to proceed cautiously, lest the fragile peace between the military at large and the new government be upset. Despite this, the new government boldly set aside the commanders' self-serving amnesty law. Predictably, this action threatened to destabilize the new democracy. Long continued describing how the commanders objected to the jurisdiction of the civilian courts over what they saw as military matters. Alfonsín eventually agreed to a compromise. He allowed the trials to be conducted first by military tribunals. However, he insisted on the proviso that if these tribunals were found to delay unnecessarily, the Buenos Aires Court of Appeals (a civilian court) would be permitted to 'assume' the cases.

Despite his best efforts at that time, Alfonsín was criticized for 'leniency' and for leaving these prosecutions solely under the jurisdiction of military courts. After a full year without a single verdict, the civilian courts took over. The Court of Appeals eventually prosecuted and convicted nine members of the Military, including General Videla and Admiral Massera.

"As you know," Long concluded. "Videla and Massera received life-long prison sentences."

For the next twenty or so minutes, Long explained how, in view of what many saw as the continuing need for Argentine society to see justice done, the lead prosecutor then opened more prosecutions against other people accused of political violence during the dictatorship. In effect, the pending Full Stop Law would mandate the end of further investigations and prosecutions. Although the proposed legislation was extremely controversial, Alfonsín's new government—which was initially opposed to the law—feared a new military *coup d'état* and eventually advanced it. Congress was going to take up the legislation in the coming weeks.

"I have assigned three seasoned reporters to cover the congressional debate," Long added. "That will not be your job. You are not ready for that." Rather, Marco's job would be to research and find everything in print in support of and opposed to the legislation.

Long explained that his editorial board had yet to formulate a definitive position on the legislation. He believed its members were almost certain to be divided. He added how, as editor-in-chief, it ultimately fell to him to balance *This Week's* reputation for reporting the news without bias and its historic concern for human welfare. Long then said that he would rely on Marco's research to guide the internal debate toward a clear and informed editorial position.

*

Marco skipped lunch and, within hours, found himself in *This Week's* vast library, sitting in front of a drab green screen scrolling through rolls of microfiche. By day's end, the contours of the underlying logic on both sides were taking shape. The work was tedious, and it left Marco with a weighty desire to sneak into another world. It was late, and he knew the nearby sauna would be filled with possibilities. Several weeks ago, there had been a young man there around his own age. Like Marco himself, he appeared to have been an athlete as a student. In a way, he reminded Marco of Agustin from the gym but taller and fairer. Marco had frequently thought about the man and hoped to see him there again.

Once inside and undressed, Marco ventured from behind the curtain of his cubicle. He looked in the steam room and the showers and then walked the corridors of cubicles, most of which were occupied. When it was apparent the young man was not there, the pressing need Marco was feeling on his way to the sauna faded. He considered going home and getting into bed but, instead, returned to the steam room. He spread his towel across the hot white tiles and lay down on his back, his eyes closed and oblivious to those around him, but with his towel slackened just enough to tease interest.

Marco listened as the steam room's fogged glass door opened and closed several times. When he looked up, he saw another man sitting on the tile bench opposite him. Marco could barely make out his features through the dimly lit, wet vapor. He felt the man looking at him. When he looked up, the man hurried wordlessly out of the room. Marco knew from years of experience how it felt to be too ashamed and nervous to do anything else. He thought about following him but instead lay back, indulging himself in the heat.

When Marco left the sauna, the same man was in the brightly lit shower room; his back turned toward the entrance. Marco hung his towel on a hook and walked to the man's side, a deliberate message because there were six other unoccupied showers in the room. The man stirred and turned, but still, he looked straight ahead. Standing naked, elbow-to-elbow, Marco could see him clearly for the first time. He was fair, thin and muscular, with light hair on his arms, legs and buttocks. *He must be a foreigner*, Marco thought.

The man turned ever-so-slightly toward Marco and unashamedly glanced at him. It became obvious the man was taking his measure, a departure from what seemed to have been his indifference of just a few moments earlier.

This man was not the young man Marco had hoped to see, but Marco nevertheless was attracted to him. Soon, other men joined them in the showers. Not wanting an 'audience', Marco turned off his shower and readied himself to leave. To his surprise, the man did the same and, pausing for a moment to wrap a towel around his waist, followed Marco into the dressing room.

The man seemed more comfortable there. He talked casually in a discrete voice as he put his clothes on. He was a taxi driver originally from Belgium. Marco asked if he came to the sauna often, although he already knew the answer; Marco came frequently enough and he had never seen him before.

The man introduced himself as Román. Soon enough, they were dressed and standing in the sauna's dimly lit bar with its tango pictures on one wall and soccer pictures on the other. It took a minute for their eyes to adjust, and when they did, they both noted that the room was empty. Marco was sure Román was going to change his mind and leave, but then Román saw that the bar had Wit beer on tap, a Belgian specialty seldom found outside Europe. At that moment, he became a different person, animated and loquacious. Román ordered for them, and explained how Wit beer was made from spices rather than hops according to a secret recipe brought to Belgium by monks. He ordered one for each of them. When Román finished his, he asked Marco if he had time for one more. Marco nodded, and Román told him to order while he used the men's room. In his absence, Marco thought about inviting him back to his apartment, but he wasn't sure how to bring it up. When Román returned, Marco simply said that he lives nearby, matter-of-factly adding *alone*. He got no response, just a smile.

    Marco took his turn for the men's room. "Will you be here when I come back?" he asked. Román assured him that he wasn't going anywhere and ordered a third beer for himself. Marco was relieved and surprised when he returned. In the back of his mind, he half expected, perhaps even wanted, his new acquaintance to have used the opportunity to slip away. He was even more surprised when Román said, "Let's go."

*

When the telephone rang the next morning, a Sunday, Marco didn't want to answer it. He woke up filled with regret. He had been having a disturbing dream about his secret life being discovered. Christina and Alberto were in the dream, and they were deeply wounded and accused him of fooling them. The compulsion Marco felt the evening before had been replaced with fear and shame. Marco thought it was a cruel twist that he should constantly desire sex so badly yet be so afraid of it. He did not know what to do about the latter or how to control the former.

The ringing phone jarred him back into the moment, and he wondered who was calling so early. While he pondered whether to answer, the ringing stopped and then started again. Marco suspected it to be Christina, and if so, she would not give up. When he picked up, it was Christina. With a bit of annoyance, she began by saying she had been trying since yesterday to reach him. "I was calling," she said with controlled patience, "to ask you to meet me at my apartment this evening." She explained that this was not a social invitation but, rather, she needed to speak with Marco about an important business matter.

When Christina hung up, he pulled the sheets over himself and went back to sleep. Two hours later, showered and dressed, he picked up the Sunday newspaper at a kiosk and went out to a café across the street. It was already early afternoon. He considered calling Christina and inviting her to meet him for coffee. They could take a nice walk and maybe talk about the evening or anything else that might be on her mind.

There was an ad in the newspaper's entertainment section for a new sauna not far from his apartment. Marco's intent took another turn; he figured he could walk to it and back, spend a couple of hours there, and still make it to Christina's by six. Marco talked to himself the whole of the twenty-minute walk. Although it was a warm afternoon, the streets were empty. As Marco approached the sauna's advertised address, he noticed several men gathered outside the door. Marco wondered what lies these men were telling themselves and whether they were the same ones he told himself.

*

Marco had come to believe Christina had magical sensory powers when it came to people. As soon as he arrived, she sensed that something was not right. "I don't know what it is," she said, "but I sense something is wrong. Do you want to talk for a bit before we join my husband?"

"No," Marco said, "I am just tired. Thanks, but let's go in." Just then, a maid informed Christina that there was a telephone call for her. "Do you mind?" Christina politely asked before leaving the room.

After a while, Alberto came into the room and announced that Christina was still detained on the telephone but would be joining them as soon as she could break away. Something about Alberto's manner suggested to Marco that this night was going to be different than the prior evening in the Darin apartment.

For one thing, the last time he was invited to dine with them, the evening started with ice-cold martinis. This evening, the bar had not been set up for guests. Soon after Christina came back, they were seated at the dining table. Christina immediately steered the conversation to the evening's business.

She explained that Reuters' editorial board, like *This Week's*, was likely to be deeply divided on the subject of the Full Stop Law (*La Ley Punto Final*). She believed the positions ultimately taken by both news outlets would be closely read and debated not only by the Argentine public but also by human rights organizations worldwide. "The next few weeks are going to be contentious. This debate is going to represent a defining act in Argentina's transition to democracy. Few laws will be as hotly debated as this one for decades to come."

Even by the standards of Christina, a woman who always spoke deliberately, her tone was exceptionally resolute and became even more so as she went on. "Argentina has many open wounds which will not be healed until we uncover the truth. There must be truth to assist families of the victims in getting closure." She finished, "The people who were most affected have a right to know at whose hands their loved ones suffered."

Once again, Alberto disagreed. In his view, the military continued to be a threat to democracy. The state had to compromise. "Granted," he said, "pardons and amnesties are objectionable, but they are necessary to remove the threat of another military takeover." He then pointed out that it was possible the facts would be too ghoulish to bear and only worsen the victims' suffering.

When it came time for Marco to speak, he pondered whether disclosing his current assignment was appropriate under the circumstances. He explained to Christina that there were aspects of his job that he did not feel at liberty to divulge. Christina expressed respect for his integrity and sense of ethics but pushed on, saying that this was an important topic she wished to discuss. When he proceeded, Marco simply said that he was doing research for Long on the subject of the Full Stop Law. "The arguments against the legislation are precisely the same arguments that were used against the Commission," he pointed out. They all knew the commission to which Marco was referring was the National Commission on the Disappeared: *CONADEP*.

When she next spoke, Christina repeated that Argentina cannot shape a future by forgetting the past atrocities committed by the regime. For emphasis, she reiterated that society needs to find a way to deal with them.

Alberto stood his philosophical ground. "There is a middle ground," he pointed out. With reference to the truth commissions used by South Africa in the 1970s, he proposed truth trials. He explained that 'truth trials' were first imagined to be a means of documenting human rights abuses. For relatives of the victims they presented an opportunity to face their loved ones' abusers. Yet, they would be unlike ordinary criminal trials in that judicial action was expressly limited to investigation and documentation, without a possibility either of prosecution or punishment. "In this regard," he added, "they are not about prosecution for crimes but about finding the truth. Perhaps the CONADEP eventually could serve this purpose."

"Perfect segue." Christina again took over. She pointed out that one of the challenges the commissioners would face was the Commission's limited timeframe of one hundred eighty days. "Six months is not much time in view of the fact that people are still afraid of the military and fear coming forward and to be identified." She added that the commissioners would need a lot of help to fulfill their mission. The next thing she said took Marco aback. "I have agreed to take a leave of absence from the Foundation to accept a temporary appointment with the Commission."

Christina gave a cat-like smile and paused for reaction. Alberto looked stunned, perhaps if only to learn this with me being present. I'm sure I just looked blank.

"As I just said," Christina repeated, "the Commission will have only six months to complete its mission. This is the reason I called you here, Marco. I need to move quickly to build out staff. There will be a lengthy investigation during which we will be focused on hearing from thousands of victims—some fifty thousand people according to human rights organizations. That will be followed by the production and publication of a report." After a suitable pause for emphasis, she said to Marco, "I would like you to join me as my senior staff assistant."

*

The conversation, now more immediate, about Christina's appointment and CONADEP's mission continued over dinner. Between the main course and dessert, Christina became personal. She folded her napkin and inquired about Marco's background, asking more personal questions about his family and his religious and political points of view. As she had before, Christina listened to Marco's short responses as if every detail was important. She went on asking personal questions for more than an hour. This time, Marco did not wish to divulge too much.

Christina eventually changed the subject somewhat abruptly and then asked in a reverently low voice whether life was difficult for him during the military's rule. "Did it affect you personally?" She sensed Marco's change of tone, which indicated that it did, and she waited patiently for a response.

"I was young, finishing school. A friend was taken off a city bus in broad daylight and never heard from again. The police said he may have escaped captivity and fled the country. But to this day, no one knows what really happened to him," Marco recounted with more emotion than he had expected. Was it because he really had never said those words out loud?

"I am sorry. It must have been hard for you. I can see that it still is. But I want you to understand my question about how difficult the work of the Commission will be.

The wounds run deep. It will be very painful for many people," she added softly.

Marco nodded and hoped this would be the end of the questions. He tried to change the subject, but Christina had another question.

"How old was he, your friend?"

"He was seventeen, the same age as me at the time."

"You must have a lot of questions about his—the euphemism is 'disappearance?'" Christina said, "There are many people looking for the answers, and that is what the Commission hopes to do. We must give them answers, reality." At that point, Christina stopped talking, and the topic of conversation was closed for the evening. Marco was left silently ruminating on Paul.

*

Marco felt triumphant. His decision to go into journalism was starting to bear fruit. Good fortune was smiling on him. He was energized and determined to make a difference in a way he personally could embrace. He recalled how, as he became better acquainted with Christina Darin, it was becoming increasingly obvious that she was going to have a significant impact on his career. Now, that was happening.

Marco went to bed excited about the assignment, but the night was restless. How was he to deal with *This Week* and his loyalty to the newspaper and to Long? He awoke several times and recalled how Christina had said the job would require their singular focus over the course of the Commission's work, and their stamina would be tested. Marco was determined to give it nothing less than his best to make himself and Christina proud.

Nevertheless, Marco awoke in the morning in the grip of compulsion. As much as he wanted to be like other men, he was tormented by the fact that he would soon sneak back into his other world. Just as he was thinking these thoughts, his telephone rang. It was Christina at her most exuberant and brisk, speaking to Marco like he imagined she spoke to her subordinates at Reuters.

Two hours later, with Marco reluctantly in tow, they were at a fashionable men's shop on Avenida Alvear. Sensing his discomfort, Christina chuckled. "Not to worry, Reuters is paying." Then, with a look that said 'brace yourself', she pointed at his frayed collar and explained that he needed to look like the part for his role at the Commission.

"You have to fit in," she coached while at the same time giving directions to the store clerks who left and soon returned with two suits, one navy blue and the other pin-stiped. Christina had Marco try on both of them, both times signaling that something was not quite right and sending him back into the dressing room to try on another one or to get back into one of the rejected suits for a second, sometimes third, time. Christina was impressed that Marco remained patient and showed no frustration. On the contrary, he treated it as a game. Christina would hand him a new suit; he unceremoniously changed into it to come out of the dressing room and turn on command front-then-back, like a toy top, for Christina's inspection. Christina complimented him on his patience.

*

Mariel Robles, one of *This Week*'s fact checkers, set up the punch bowl. Manning baked a cake for the occasion, which she placed on the table next to it. In big letters made of blue icing, the cake read; *BUENA SUERTE MARCO.*

Staffers were drifting in, some staying just long enough to shake Marco's hand and congratulate him, others staying for the libations. One of the editors joked that even *This Week's* society page editor was on hand to cover the party, a dubious honor. This got a laugh and prompted Manning to report that Long himself would also be coming but, as usual, was delayed.

The attention was making Marco feel a bit sentimental and embarrassed. After all, he had only been at *This Week* for a short while. Moreover, everyone he worked with was very nice. They put him in the pool initially and then gave him increasingly challenging and interesting assignments, each an opportunity to prove himself. He had come to understand his treatment was not typical. And he also had come to see *This Week* for what it was. For all its venerable history, it was really just a periodical produced and published every week by a dedicated, albeit aging, staff that was half eccentric and half brilliant—often at the same time!

There was a small stack of that week's edition on a table just inside the door. Marco was glancing at the front page. One of the editors saw Marco perusing it. "Poor time to read," he said in jest.

Marco laughed and looked up. "You're absolutely right," he replied: "I was just looking to see if we are reporting anything about the Commission."

At that moment, Long joined the party. He announced that he only had a few minutes and he would like to say a few words. Everyone fell silent. "It was immediately apparent to me that young Campora here is going to be a fine journalist." Then, turning to Marco, he became personal: "Your re-writes brought the perfect grammar of the *Nacionale*-educated to our veteran reporters' copy. I wish now that we had more for you to do while you were with us, and we had more time to get to know eachother." Marco blushed, and everyone else broke into applause.

Long finished with an invitation. "Kid, you are off to do an important job. But it's temporary. Don't forget that there will be a job waiting for you here."

*

The message light on Marco's answering machine was blinking when he returned home. The message was from his brother, Santiago. Santiago was living in Washington, D.C. He was an economist with a prestigious think tank. Sr. Campora had arranged the position for his eldest son during negotiations with American officials over the restructuring of Argentina's sovereign debt. Marco instantly recalled how the brothers were very close growing up, but now they talked infrequently and somewhat superficially.

Santiago delivered the news. Marco's father had died suddenly hours before from a massive stroke. Santiago seemed surprisingly at ease. Sr. Campora had been in failing health for almost a year and had almost died months before when a bad bronchial infection turned into pneumonia.

It seemed to Marco that his father would have wanted to die if the alternative was paralysis and impaired speech beyond comprehension. He could not imagine him as a shadow of his former very-in-control self. He didn't share these thoughts with his brother. There would be plenty of time for that in the coming days. Rather, he inquired about their mother's state. Santiago assured him that he had spoken with her on the telephone, and she seemed to be 'holding up'. Marco reported that he would travel to San Isidro that evening. Santiago said he would be there as soon as he could get a flight from Washington.

As Marco waited for a bus, he felt a peculiar angst. *That was normal,* he thought. After all, he just learned that his father had died. Yet, that wasn't exactly it. It had more to do with what he was not feeling. Marco had a complicated relationship with his father. He always knew his father had a dark side and felt he had become brutish in recent years. He was sure Santiago and his younger brother, Juan, would feel differently. They always were the 'dutiful' sons. Their relationships within the family, particularly with Sr. Campora, were the stabilizing force of their lives. When the three spoke of Sr. Campora, it was as though Marco and his brothers had grown up in different households.

The bus took its usual route through slow traffic, eventually coming to the end of the line at Estación Retiro. Marco thought about the days ahead. In contrast to Santiago, who had recently been home for a short stay, Marco had not been home for a visit for almost a year.

Even though he knew it was his family duty to be there for the funeral services, even then, he was planning to keep his visit short.

Marco's reluctance to visit San Isidro traced back to his days when the family, especially Sr. Campora, controlled every aspect of his life. Granted, that was a dangerous time. The generals were running the country. But it was more than that. Marco wasn't free to speak for himself. Sometimes, it felt as though he wasn't free even to think for himself. Now, he feared that too many nights back home under the family's influence would in some way return him to the turmoil of his adolescence.

As soon as Marco passed through the front door, Sra. Campora emerged from the drawing room to greet him. Her greeting was direct.

"There you are," she said. "We've been wondering." It was not the warmest greeting, but Marco excused it under the circumstances.

Then, pointing to the double doors that led to his father's dark study, she said, "Juan is in there with Father." And asked if Marco wished to see him now.

Marco shook his head. "I'll go in later."

Marco and his mother slowly walked together through the dark, paneled hall. Neither said anything to the other. Marco wanted to say he was sorry, but it seemed superfluous.

"There are calling arrangements to be made. I will need your help. Can you handle that?" his mother finally said.

"Yes, I can manage," Marco replied.

Marco had been hoping it would be a private memorial service for just the immediate family and a few of his father's closest relatives. His angst was increasing by the moment. "So many people will insist on coming," his mother said. "There are your father's relatives. Members of the Club will want to come. And then there's the officialdom of your father's protégés and colleagues in the military and government who must be formally received." Marco inwardly groaned.

As they passed the study, they met Juan in the hall. He seemed both tragic and cross. There was no greeting, embrace or sympathy expressed by either brother.

"Where have you been?" Juan asked, barely masking irritation.

Marco did not answer. Sra. Campora saved him.

"Marco and I were just reminiscing as family so often does at times like these." She led them, her middle and youngest sons, away from the study and into the drawing room.

"You must be tired," she said to Marco.

Marco sat momentarily, then rose to fix drinks. "Who'd like one?"

"I might take a light one," Sra. Campora said.

"Nothing for me," Juan quickly added and then slowly backed out of the room.

Marco brought the highball to his mouth. Evening was approaching, and the setting sun cast long shadows across the floor and up the opposite wall. The house was silent except for the muffled sound of soft footsteps on the hardwood floor above. He found the drink and the noise soothing and leaned back into the over-stuffed chair. Here, in years past, Sr. and Sra. Campora had drinks before every meal. Then, Sra. Campora usually passed what was the day's only quiet hour by herself, going over the occurrences that passed for daily life in the Campora home.

Sr. Campora used the library as his personal office. However, his business or what he actually did for a living was never quite clear to any of the three boys. His dealings were strictly private—known only to him and the man in the cracked painting that still hung on the wall. When Marco was growing up, 'Father's study' was the one room in the house that no one entered without invitation or first knocking on the door, not even Sra. Campora. It was a sign of the toll pneumonia and the stroke took on him that his private sanctuary had become a sick room. His various nurses and an occasional doctor casually came and went, something that would have been unquestionably forbidden while he was still in control. In this way, and probably in so many other ways, he had been dying for almost a year.

Marco got up and quietly crossed the hall. He knocked softly on the study door, mindful of the irony in this. Fortunately, the room was empty save for this father's body, which was laid out on a narrow hospital bed under white sheets that were neatly drawn up to his chin. The bed had been squeezed against a wall of books that Marco wondered if his father had ever actually read. The massive desk Marco had always revered was covered with plastic and a linen cloth, apparently to protect the wood. The room smelled vaguely of pipe smoke and antiseptics. The old painting of the stern man, apparently Marco's grandfather, watched over the scene.

Marco stood rather uncomfortably at the foot of the bed, not sure what he should be doing or even feeling. He rarely had anything to say to his father in recent years. He saw no point in saying anything then. He thought he should at least say a prayer, but none came to mind. For a moment, he regretted his lack of a religious tradition for, surely, he should have known some kind of prayer for the departed. Not knowing what else to do, Marco stared blankly at the lifeless body.

Marco was trembling lightly when Juan appeared at his side. Juan put a hand on his shoulder, the first brotherly thing he had done since Marco's arrival.

"How are you getting along?" Juan asked, his voice low as if to reinforce the notion the dead have gone to their eternal rest and were not to be disturbed.

"I am getting along fine," he said evenly. He could not share with Juan the emotional confusion he was feeling.

"You cannot be 'fine,'" he replied pointedly. "Father just died."

Marco didn't want an argument and rephrased his response, "I am doing fine under the circumstances."

"Are you?" Juan pressed.

"Yes, yes, of course," Marco replied impatiently. "What is the point of pretending otherwise?"

In the silence that followed, Marco knew what was coming and braced for it. Juan predictably returned to his long-held and seldom-forgotten grudge.

"You were his favorite. Santiago and I both accepted it." A tone of anger and resentment had crept into Juan's voice.

After a pause that lasted uncomfortably long, Marco replied.

"Maybe that was true for a time."

"You know Santiago was the one who told Father?" Juan sort of asked.

"Is that a question?" Marco asked, his own anger rising. "I think I know what you are referring to, but please tell me just what he supposedly told him?"

"That Paul was queer."

"Is that what you thought?" Marco asked defensively.

"I didn't care one way or another. It didn't matter to me what you and Paul were up to back then."

Marco said nothing.

After a deep breath, Juan said he would be retiring to his room. It had become obvious that their conversation was going to become an argument. Juan backed out of the room, leaving Marco alone with his thoughts and memories and his father's body. He was tired but now too agitated to turn in. It had been a long afternoon. Glancing at his watch, he saw that it was going on eight o'clock and realized that he had not eaten for almost twelve hours. As he prepared to exit the study, there was a soft knock on the door.

"May I come in?"

Marco realized at that moment that his mother had just become a widow. Dressed all in a widow's black, she seemed calm, serene even.

"Are you doing all right, Mother?"

"I'll be fine," she answered and then lowered herself into one of the chairs at Sr. Campora's bedside. "It was not a shock, you know, not really. Your father had not been himself for some time. Many thought it was because of the pneumonia. But not me. I think he knew he was becoming irrelevant like other once-powerful men of his age. He felt that deeply. Perhaps, in some way, he looked forward to the end of life, maybe even willed it."

"Do you think that's possible?" she asked rhetorically of no one in particular.

She did not wait for an answer. She went on, "Your father became deeply depressed." Then, after a pause, she sighed as if she had lost her train of thought. "Oh well, what does it matter now? He's gone," her words heavy and resolute.

She looked up at Marco. Marco closed his eyes and nodded, doing his best to look appropriately bereaved. He bent over and took his mother's hand in his. "Would you like me to sit up with you?" he asked in a tone that was both sincere and concerned.

"No, no," she replied with assurances that she was grateful for the offer. "You need time alone to come to terms with your own memories. And you must be hungry! Josephina will make you something. She has prepared your old room for you as well. Will you eat in the kitchen, or shall I have her bring it up?"

Marco thanked her and said, "I feel better knowing you will be all right."

*

One of his mother's sleeping pills helped Marco through the night. It was almost noon by the time he went down for breakfast, much later than expected. The family's long-time housemaid, Josephina, reported that two men had come to the house and removed Sr. Campora's body to the funeral home earlier that morning. She offered to fix him some scrambled eggs. Marco asked about his mother and if she had eaten any breakfast. She hadn't. As far as Josephina knew, she fixed herself some tea and went directly to the study to meet Juan and the funeral directors. Marco found his mother in the vacant study, sitting alone. The door was open. Her back was turned. She was looking through the French doors to the garden beyond. Out of respect for her privacy, Marco stepped lightly.

"Uh, hmm."

Sra. Campora turned with a start. "Oh, good morning. You seem to have had a full night's rest. Shall I ask Josephina to bring tea or something?"

"No, Mother, I just had a cup of coffee. I don't want anything else for now."

"And you," he asked. "I understand you haven't had any breakfast?"

"I'll eat something at lunchtime," she responded softly. "Right now, I want to tidy up this room."

"Shouldn't we leave that to Josephina?" Marco asked.

"No," she answered. "I want to do it myself."

Marco pretended not to notice that she had been crying. He watched as she stripped the bed while he dragged two heavy chairs from the bedside to their usual places in front of the fireplace. Within the span of an hour, they agreed that their work was done. The room looked more like its former, foreboding self.

As they readied to leave the room, Josephina came to the door and announced that Santiago's plane had landed and he should arrive within the hour. He had flown from Washington via Houston on a thirteen-hour overnight flight. Marco was planning to promptly confront him with Juan's claim that Santiago told his father Paul was queer. He was anxious to know why he thought that and how his father reacted. But Santiago was very tired when he finally arrived. He greeted Marco and Juan and, after briefly checking up on his mother, announced that he was going directly to his old room for a shower and a nap. Marco's questions would have to wait.

*

Sra. Campora and Santiago were the first to enter the chapel, Sra. Campora on her elder son's arm. She was wearing an elegant but old-fashioned black dress, black gloves and a *mantilla*. As the new widow passed, row after row of men reverently removed their hats. Relations, friends, retired military and government officials hushed and turned to look at her. She didn't stop at the Campora's usual pew. Rather, she took her customary seat between Santiago and Marco in the pew reserved for the immediate family. Juan sat at Marco's right, ramrod straight, eyes fixed on the coffin.

The priest stood and signaled the start of the service. All rose.

"In the name of the Father, and of the Son…"

Sra. Campora reached over to Marco and gently patted his shoulder.

"We are gathered here to remember…"

Sra. Campora stood tall, occasionally lifting her eyes to glance at the flag-draped pall. The comparatively simple oak box that rested on it contained the remains of the man to whom she had devoted her adult life. She was there for him, serene and proud, as she had been for the past forty-two years.

When the service was over, the family left as they had entered. Sra. Campora and Santiago led, followed by Marco and Juan. Back at the house, they were greeted by Josephina and several other servants who had been hired for the occasion, all looking neat in their black dresses and starched white collars. Sra. Campora asked Josephina to take her up to her bedroom, where she intended to rest for a short while. Juan offered to accompany her. She declined, saying she wished to shut her eyes before their guests started arriving.

Marco invited Santiago to join him in the study where he immediately poured himself another highball. He offered one to Santiago. Marco noticed that Santiago was unsettled. He thought back to the time before he went away to school when he and Santiago were close. So much had changed between them.

Santiago started right in. "Juan told me that you now know."

"What you told Father?" Marco asked.

"Yes, you know what I am talking about." *Here we go.*

"You cannot forgive him, can you?"

"And just what is there for me to forgive?" Marco asked as evenly and coyly as he could.

"Oh, don't pretend you don't know what I am talking about. He drove Paul away."

Marco took a sip of bourbon. A familiar tension was mounting above his eyes.

"As long as we are on the subject, I would like to know what made you think Paul was queer and why you told Father without talking to me first."

"Things like the fact that you locked yourselves in your bedroom when he stayed over."

"That's it?" Marco was incredulous. "Because I locked my bedroom door?"

"There was more. I saw the way Paul looked at you. His eyes were always on you. He idolized you."

"If you had asked me, I might have acknowledged that Paul sometimes seemed infatuated with me. You mistook that for lust, which I don't believe it was. Paul's life was different than ours. He wanted to be me."

Marco repeated his question. "So why *didn't* you talk to me first?"

"I am not sure; I just didn't. I thought Father would know best how to handle the situation. I admit now that I was wrong, and I am sorry."

Santiago signaled that was it. He did not wish to continue the discussion. On his way out of the room, he reminded Marco that their father had always acted in all of the brothers' best interests.

When Santiago was gone, Marco opened a window. A sheer curtain billowed in the light breeze. The family's guests would start arriving soon. Noon was drawing near, and the bright sun was warm and inviting. Years of anger struggled for release. Marco wondered what purpose was served by dragging up the topic of Paul again, particularly on this occasion. *He vanished one afternoon. A lot of people vanished at that time. I may never know what happened to him.*

*

Juan was at the front door dutifully greeting the families' guests as they entered, one by one. He was naturally warm, gracious and affable in his role.

After a short while, the main hall was filled to near capacity. The servers were busy with drinks and light snacks as the guests talked among themselves in small circles of relatives, Club members and former colleagues.

Some of the faces were familiar to Marco, but he couldn't place others. Indeed, for the first time in his life, Marco felt oddly like a distant relative. Sr. Campora had few relatives and even fewer close friends. It seemed everyone in his life, except his wife and children, had their purpose, and that purpose usually had to do with business in one way or another.

There was a congregation from the *Mecon*, the ministry where Sr. Campora had been a long-time and well-respected deputy. His position was a political appointment. During the Perón presidency, it carried a lot of prestige and, not incidentally, quite a lot of power. It had to do with foreign contracts, including the procurement of military hardware. In those days, the minister was a close confidant of the president, and Sr. Campora had worked closely with Peron. However, in the years just prior to Sr. Campora's retirement, ministers came and went as frequently as the occupants of the Casa Rosada.

There was also a number of military men, some active but most retired. Marco never quite knew how his father truthfully felt about the generals or to what extent he was 'in' with them. He never heard his father complain about any of them, but then again, that was not his style. If he had any such views, he would never have divulged them.

*

Marco took another sleeping pill and slept that night on his old bed. Looking around the room, he took inventory of his childhood pride, a collection of ribbons and trophies, all collecting dust. He thought about a recurring dream involving Paul that, for years, would keep him awake some nights. The dream was always the same. Paul would glance longingly at Marco as Marco rushed to catch the Mitre train that would take him home. In this dream, Marco would often sense Paul's lonesomeness, and the prospect of sleeping together in the same room excited him. Marco always woke up before anything happened between the boys.

At breakfast, Sra. Campora invited Marco to take a walk in the garden. They walked in unsettling silence for a while. Sra. Campora was the first to speak. Surprisingly, she reported that Santiago brought up Paul's name in one of their conversations. She thought that was peculiar and wanted to know if he had mentioned Paul in his conversations with Marco. As they walked along the moist garden path, she said that she had always liked Paul. Marco bridled at the thought of how much the family must have been discussing his private life and his friendship.

Sra. Campora asked if Marco had ever questioned Paul's sexuality. In the brief exchange that ensued, she boldly used the word 'homosexual' twice. Caught off guard, Marco sputtered that the possibility had occurred to him, but it didn't matter. "Well, Santiago thought he might be," she said obviously studying Marco for his reaction. She added that Sr. Campora was sure he was and did not like the idea of Marco spending time with him.

When they reached the house, Sra. Campora said she supposed Marco would be leaving soon to return to his job and life in Buenos Aires. She asked a bit gloomily, "Are you happy with your life, Marco? Do you have friends in Buenos Aires?"

"Yes, I am, and I do," he answered. "Does that surprise you?"

"No, you always did have friends. But you never speak of them."

"They would not interest you, Mother."

"Is that really it? Should I not be the judge of that?"

The uncharacteristic intimacy and candor of their conversation took Marco aback. He then assured her that he was perfectly happy and changed the subject.

*

The following morning, Marco found himself back in his father's library. He wanted to find some small thing to remember him by, something he could take home. For reasons he could not summon, he was drawn to the leather chair behind the mysterious desk. He slowly sat down. It was something none of them would have done during his father's lifetime. Someone had pushed back the plastic from the desktop. Marco guardedly opened a drawer. Then, he went through the few other drawers that were not locked. Everything seemed to be just as neat and organized as his father had left it. It reflected a life of everything in its place. On one side of the massive desk, there were three drawers containing files for the usual family things such as household receipts, insurance and medical records. Marco moved from drawer to drawer, perusing the file labels without removing or reading any of their contents. He promised himself that he might make time to go through them someday, possibly with the assistance of Juan and Santiago.

When Marco swiveled around in the worn leather desk chair, he noticed a relatively thick file lying by itself on the credenza behind him. He was sure it had not been there two days ago when he helped his mother clean the room. At first glance, it didn't appear to be one of his father's files, all of which were kept in standard manila folders. This was a drab green folio wrapped with an elastic band tightly stretched around it. When he turned it over, the label stopped him cold: Paul Casales.

Marco was shocked to see that his father—or someone—was so interested in Paul and wondered why this file was left out in the open. Taking a deep breath, he carefully removed the elastic tie. He started to go through it right then, but most of its contents were scribbled notes on yellow paper with redacted blocks of black ink. Marco was tempted to go through it right there but thought better of it, deciding instead to take it with him. He wondered if anyone would notice it was missing.

*

Marco returned to Buenos Aires the following day on an evening train carrying the yet-to-be-studied green file. His landlady met him at the door upon his arrival at his apartment. He had had a few beers on the way home. He was slightly buzzed and immediately assumed there was some kind of problem.

"A man asked me to hand this to you," she said as she handed him a sealed envelope.

He assumed it was a sympathy message, probably from Christina. The envelope was blank on the outside. Inside, the short letter was written on a piece of fine stationery with no letterhead and signed by Sr. Pablo Lupi. The handwriting was unsteady, as though written by someone elderly.

I am a friend of your late father. We worked together on a number of projects over the years. I am in Buenos Aires for the funeral and will soon return to Brasilia. I would be honored if you would be my guest for dinner, as I did not have the chance to talk with you at the funeral. I will be at Tomasino's this evening. If you are so inclined, kindly meet me there at twenty-one hundred hours. If I do not hear from you, I will quite understand. My deepest condolences for your loss. That was it. No reason was given. The scrawled signature was barely decipherable.

The restaurant was almost full when Marco arrived. He had left early and walked. It was a cool day, typical weather for the capital.

The *maître d'* found Lupi's reservation and, after informing Marco that he was the first to arrive, asked whether he would like to be seated or to wait in the bar.

Marco knew Tomasino's. It was a favorite midday destination for reporters and political types. When they were having a casual lunch or just wanting to relax for the occasional meal on their own, they chose the ground floor grill. But, for more serious business they usually favored the grander and more private second floor. Marco asked whether Lupi had indicated a preference. He had not, so Marco asked to be seated on the grill level.

Marco ordered a bourbon neat and waited. Before the waiter could deliver it, Marco noticed the *maître d'* leading a tall, middle-aged man into the room. Something made Marco tense as the two approached.

"Thank you," the silver-haired man said as he palmed a folded bill into the *maître d*'s hand. Looking directly at his host, Marco rose with an outstretched hand.

"Splendid," Lupi exclaimed as he took and shook Marco's hand.

Lupi settled into the chair opposite Marco. The awkward silence was broken by the waiter, who appeared and immediately asked Lupi if he would like a cocktail.

"Yes, of course," he replied. "You must join me in having a cocktail, Marco. What's your pleasure?"

Just as Marco began to say he had ordered a bourbon, Lupi said, "bourbon will be perfect." Without further consultation, he ordered an Old Fashioned and specified a brand unfamiliar to Marco.

"Have you eaten here before?" Lupi asked. "This must be familiar ground for *This Week's* people."

"No, I haven't," Marco replied. "But I think my former boss comes here a lot, I suppose, for the reasons you are implying. May I ask how you knew I worked for the paper?"

Lupi turned toward Marco with a coy smile. Marco knew he should say something conversational, but he was confounded. He felt like he was at the side of a swimming pool, trying to coax himself into the cold water. He did not want to talk about himself. Rather, he was anxious for Lupi to tell him what this was about and, just as pressing, who he was! The best Marco could do was suggest they study the menu and say, "After we order, Sr. Lupi, perhaps you will tell me why you asked me here and how well you knew my father." Lupi again looked at Marco with that smile, and after fixing his glasses to each ear, he studied the menu. When the waiter returned, they ordered pork for Lupi and short ribs for Marco.

"Will you have some wine?" Lupi asked hopefully. "They appear to have several nice ones. May I choose?"

"Yes, of course," Marco responded without expression.

Lupi ordered a fine Malbec Reserva and handed the wine list back to the waiter.

After what seemed like an eternity, Lupi spoke. "Well, it is quite nice of you to meet me this evening," Marco responded with something vague but polite about feeling obliged to do so, although, at that very moment, he wished he was off somewhere on his own having a beer.

Lupi began to explain. He was a bureaucrat in the same ministry as Marco's father. He actually was two levels below Sr. Campora in rank, but apparently, they were good friends. Lupi had been in the same position for more than twenty years, and, as you would expect of someone with that kind of experience, his institutional knowledge was considered indispensable. Or so he said with no hint of modesty. The wine and food were served, and Lupi continued talking about himself while eating unabashedly.

Marco assessed Lupi's life story to be a syllabus of normalcy, if not mundane. He and his wife had been married for forty-one years. They had three grown children, a girl and two boys, each of whom graduated from university. They had a lovely garden in which his wife still grew her own herbs, and on-and-on he droned. Marco was glad to let him go on talking, as he was disinclined to talk about his own life.

Lupi finally paused and looked directly at Marco. "Listen to me jabbering on and on like this. As if you care." Again, the half-smile. "I am afraid I have not given you an opportunity to tell me anything about you. Do you ever get back to San Isidro?"

Marco was not sure how much he wanted to reveal in response to this question—or any of Lupi's queries. The journalist in him felt reluctant to respond to such a personal inquiry. The true answer would have been, *No, I have come to dislike many things about San Isidro: its materialism, sense of entitlement, its politics*. He was not about to explain. Instead, he simply said that he had his own life here in Buenos Aires, which kept him quite busy.

"That's right," Lupi exclaimed. "How rude of me to ramble without asking how you are getting on at the Commission. I understand the position suits you very well." Marco was annoyed that Lupi seemed to know so much about him.

Lupi politely waited for Marco's response. Marco did not say more. He did not want to be subjected to an interview that he did not want to have. But Lupi pressed on.

"May I ask which events the Commission is going to focus on?"

As he again patiently paused for Marco's response, Lupi cut a last piece of meat and slowly brought it to his mouth, followed by a sip of wine. He obviously was willing to wait for his answer.

"As I understand it, my first assignment will be to oversee the staff tasked with the review of military files. These may shed light on the fate of the missing persons." He explained that was about all he was at liberty to say on the subject.

"Humm," Lupi said ruminatively, "I am afraid that is going to be quite a difficult task, although I am not sure why?"

Marco was tempted to contradict him but decided he did not wish to discuss the matter or disclose even more. So, instead, he suggested they change the subject.

"Yes, perhaps we should," Lupi agreed. "But before we do, I feel it's my obligation to inform you that your father and I saw no point to the Commission. We firmly opposed its formation. The military's ranks are at a very dangerous low. It does not need another so-called 'truth commission.' The military must boost morale and reestablish command control." Lupi's tone was didactic and matter-of-fact.

"It is curious that you should speak of *morale*," Marco said, realizing that Lupi and the wine were drawing him further into the conversation than he cared to go. But he continued anyway. "I am not saying soldiers do not have a difficult job. However, I do believe the tactics employed to implement the Process were 'manifestly illegal,' and these must be examined."

"And who is to say which tactics were 'manifestly illegal?'" Lupi asked.

"Well, I rather like the way an Israeli court answered that question in the trial of Adolf Eichmann. The judge's words are still quoted today. I'm paraphrasing here, but the ruling states that the distinguishing mark of a 'manifestly illegal' activity is that above such activity should fly a black flag saying 'Prohibited'! Throughout the time of our own military dictatorship, a 'black flag' was hanging over the ESMA. But people, presumably like my father and you, blindly supported the military and refused to see it."

If Lupi was offended, he did not show it. Yet, an oppressive, momentary silence settled over the table. Then, Lupi started speaking again. "The common argument in this matter presents a dilemma from which there is no escape. Do you see that?"

"No," Marco answered with a weary sigh. "I don't see it that way."

Lupi waited politely, then went back to an earlier question that Marco thought he had successfully evaded. "I would still like to know why you infrequently visited San Isidro during your father's last years. I know your father missed you, to say nothing of your mother."

Marco did not want to be confrontational, but he said such a question was rather personal and private and asked why this concerned Lupi.

Lupi continued prying. "By any chance, does it have anything to do with that young friend of yours? What was his name? Casales, I think?" Marco now saw Lupi's smile as smug and condescending.

Marco was stunned by Lupi's bold presumption and was sure this was the real reason for his invitation. He tightened. Lupi waited for his answer. Tiny beads of perspiration formed on the back of Marco's neck and forehead. He wanted to wipe them with his napkin, but his hand had begun to tremble with anger.

Lupi pressed on. "I heard that your friend moved away and got married. To Australia, or Spain, I think. I cannot recall. I talked to so many after the funeral. But, of course, you knew this, didn't you?"

Marco hoped his face didn't reflect his shock or rising ire. Fortunately, he was saved from reacting because Lupi continued without pausing to catch his breath or take another sip of wine. "I keep forgetting that he was rumored to have been arrested by the police, and you joined his mother on something of a campaign that terribly embarrassed your poor father. But you must know of that, too." Lupi's tone had become sardonic with a harsh edge. "What did become of the 'Mother?'"

Marco finally spoke up, "Sra. Casales, the 'Mother,' as you put it, died several years back."

"Oh?" Lupi exclaimed dispassionately. "I hope you are not going to tell me she died of a broken heart."

Marco responded flatly. "I think the official cause of death was ruled at the time to be a suicide."

For once, Lupi seemed to be at a loss for words. He picked up his nearly empty wine glass and drained the very little left. Finally, he looked at Marco uncomfortably. But before Lupi could say anything, Marco spoke again.

"You were saying?" Marco asked, "Something about Paul being abroad, perhaps to Australia or Spain. How and why would you know that?"

"Oh, yes," he said, again trying to sip from the now-empty glass. "It was something your older brother said."

If Lupi's intent in the meeting was to wield a verbal dagger on behalf of his old friend and comrade, Marco was determined not to let him see him bleed.

*

Autumn was settling in. The days were becoming warmer. Marco was as preoccupied with his work at the Commission as Christina had predicted. Yet, he thought often about Román. Though he had visited the Full Sauna on several occasions, he saw no more of him. During one of these visits, Marco learned from the attendant at the admissions kiosk that Román had been back to the sauna on a couple of occasions. The attendant also told him that his real name was Pedro and that, like Marco, he also might be a journalist working, perhaps, for a newspaper. Marco wrote his telephone number on a blank piece of paper and asked the attendant to give it to Pedro the next time he saw him.

Pedro, aka Román, rang Marco at his apartment a few days later. He nervously introduced himself and asked if this was a convenient time to talk. Marco was also nervous. He tried to picture Pedro on the other end of the line. He imagined he was in his thirties but had only a vague memory of his appearance. For the next forty minutes, they swapped newspaper stories and otherwise had a conversation about each other's interests that gradually became more relaxed. Marco found himself longing to see Pedro again. At the end of the conversation, Pedro asked Marco if he would meet him for a drink at the Alvear Palace Hotel. They agreed to meet the following evening at eight-thirty.

Pedro was waiting when Marco arrived. He turned and smiled as Marco approached and asked if he would mind sitting at the bar. Pedro's appearance was much as Marco remembered it, although now face-to-face, he thought Pablo was closer to forty. No matter; he was handsome and had obviously put effort into what he was wearing. Marco took that as a compliment. Marco liked the way he smiled. It was genuine and warm.

They talked about the new administration and their respective jobs. Pedro was a good listener. He listened intently as Marco told him how much he had enjoyed working at *This Week* and that he planned to return to that job at the completion of his assignment with the CONADEP. When Pedro asked questions, Marco tried to answer them honestly but discretely without revealing too much. All the while, Pedro smiled and listened attentively. At the mention of the Commission, Pedro interrupted to tell Marco that he was going to be covering the Commission's deliberations himself.

When Pedro asked Marco about his own experiences during the Process, Marco told the truth. He explained that a good friend had been taken off a crowded city bus in the late afternoon in front of many other riders, some of whom heard him scream his name and later contacted his mother. He told how later he helped Paul's mother spend weeks filing missing person reports with police precincts and the government, all of which advised them that they had no record of his arrest and supposed that he probably had fled the country like so many others. Marco thought Paul had been targeted because of his political views or, maybe, because he had homosexual tendencies. He had never said the part about Paul's tendencies out loud or even allowed himself to dwell on that possibility, but he supposed Pedro would understand.

Pedro gave a knowing, sympathetic nod. "And now, your search for information has become a quest for justice?"

"I still have slight hopes of finding Paul," Marco explained how he had sifted through many files as part of his job with the Commission and how he was told recently that Paul may have fled to another country, possibly Australia or Spain. "I do not put much faith in that possibility, but when my job at the Commission is finished, I plan to look further into it, Marco said. "If I could get more information about his fate, it would help me enormously." Marco sensed that Pedro had a similar story of his own, but he did not pursue it. He felt both of them had already said enough on the subject.

After two drinks, they agreed the Palace was a bit too grand and decided to move to a nearby neighborhood bar where they would be more comfortable. It was a warm night, and the sun was still up, so they agreed to walk the mile or so distance. The conversation became more about each other's lives. Pedro was impressed by Marco's revelation that he was raised in San Isidro and the few tidbits of information he shared about his family. He wanted to know more. But Marco had his own questions. He asked about Pedro's life. When did he first know he was gay; had he ever been with a woman, and when did he start visiting the saunas?

Aimlessly and uncharacteristically, especially for Marco, they continued discussing all sorts of personal things. For Marco, it seemed to be the first time the words flowed freely with few pauses. Marco enjoyed Pedro's attention and the sound of his voice. He wanted to go home with Pedro. But meeting someone like Pedro was new to him. He was conflicted. Would they have sex? Would they both feel disconnected and despondent afterward? Would Marco be expected to leave or stay the night? He sensed there were new rules.

Pedro took charge as soon as they arrived at his apartment. He mixed two drinks without asking Marco what he would like and once again raised a glass, this time in a silent toast. Neither Pedro nor Marco touched their drink. Without saying a word, Marco placed his head in Pedro's lap, a gesture to which Pedro responded by lightly rubbing Marco's chest and neck. They lay like that for some time before Pedro lifted Marco's head and kissed him.

"Shall we go into the other room?" Pedro murmured.

Pedro's bedroom looked comfortable and attractive. Marco sat on a chair and watched as Pedro adjusted the lamplights. He presumed he would be sleeping here in the bedroom with Pedro, but he was not sure. He said nothing.

Pedro was also quiet. He excused himself to use the adjoining bathroom. Marco heard him turn on the shower and sat back, listening to the water. When Pedro came out, there was a white towel wrapped tightly around his waist. Marco could tell he was partly aroused, and, not knowing what to do next, he froze. When Pedro asked if Marco wanted to join him in his bed, Marco's mind was racing with nervous anticipation.

Once in bed, Pedro immediately moved toward Marco without saying anything. They embraced, and Pedro ran his warm hand up and down Marco's back and then over his buttocks. Marco feared the moment when Pedro would reach between his legs. There was none of the excitement and pure sensation that he felt when he was tricking anonymously at the sauna.

When the moment finally came, Pedro asked Marco if he was sure he wanted to go on.

"Yes," Marco said, followed by, "I am sure." Then, after a few moments of silence, he added, "There is something inside of me that makes it difficult for me to actually enjoy intimacy with anyone, male or female." Marco explained that he longed for intimacy, but sometimes—often—when it is offered, he shies away, vulnerable and afraid.

"But you occasionally have sex with men at the sauna, don't you?"

"Yes, but not as often as you might think. And that is just about the sex," Marco replied practically in a hush and sat up. "And, anyway, that's totally different. The thrill is the unknowing and danger, not the sex. This is different and new to me. I like you and want you to like me. This has consequences."

Pedro sat up and lit a cigarette. He got out of bed and wrapped himself in his robe, which he pulled tightly around himself. He seemed distant and confused. "We should sleep," he said.

Spain
1986

With the initial publication of *Nunca Mas* (Never Again), the Commission's work was finished. Its massive report compiled some fifty thousand pages of depositions from which it had cobbled together detailed documentation of the military's treatment of its captives and attempted to shed light on their fates.

In the days leading up to its release, the Commission's final official duty, there was time for the staff to contemplate the magnitude of the assignment they had undertaken and completed. The somber gravity of the moment seemed to have come over everyone in the Commission's office. Instead of ringing telephones and tapping keyboards, there was an odd silence. It was as if each person in the room was ruminating over her or his own accomplishment and contribution to the herculean result. For his part, Marco also was thinking about Paul, trying to recapture him. For countless hours, he had searched through piles of documents for any information about the missing. At the beginning of every day, he hoped that day he would discover a folder bearing the name 'Casales, Paul'.

Even Christina's demeanor had changed. At her best, her manner was always sharp, decisive and authoritative.

During those waning post-publication days, however, she seemed to grasp the staff's mood and the heft of their work. Her intensity slackened, and her demeanor softened. Even the indefatigable and imposing Christina Darin seemed to be liberated and freely expressed gratitude to the members of the staff, individually and as a group. She was planning to return to her job at Reuters and invited Marco to join her there. Marco was equally ready to move on to the next chapter in his own life. However, despite the good fortune of having opportunities at both Reuters and *This Week*, he was a bit unsure about the path he would follow.

*

Despite going through reams of information about tens of thousands of victims, Marco's work on the Commission resulted in no proof that Paul was dead. Now that its work was done and its office closed, he found himself pulled in another direction, almost as if by a magnet. After sharing a short version of his reasons, he explained to Long that he had to settle some things in his own mind and informed him that he needed a brief break before returning to *This Week*.

After hastily making the necessary arrangements, two days later, Marco boarded a flight to Madrid, followed by a train to Seville. As the AVE grinded to a stop at Seville's Santa Justa station, Marco was thinking about the series of events that had brought him there. Against Christina's advice (she thought it was a fool's errand), he felt compelled to make the journey. The idea of coming to Seville had been percolating in Marco's mind for some time, and his work at the Commission only focused on it. It started with Sr. Lupi's comment about Paul possibly being in Spain. But the ultimate inducement was a handwritten note he found while going through the odd file he found in his father's study. It simply read: *Spain 30/05/1981, Last known address: Hotel Doña María, Calle Don Remondo, 19, Sevilla.*

Marco initially thought about booking the Hotel Doña María itself, but he eventually thought better of it and booked another nearby hotel. Once in Seville, Marco was glad he did. He was afraid of chancing upon Paul and thought it wise to avoid him until he was emotionally prepared to do so. Among many other things, he wondered if he would recognize Paul and whether they still would have anything in common. He realized he had no idea what he would say to him. He even allowed himself to ponder whether he really wanted to see Paul and what he expected to accomplish by doing so. He decided that he did not want to come upon him until he sorted these things out.

*

"Welcome, Señor Campora," the smiling desk clerk said and then asked for his passport. It was late evening. The day had been warm and still was. The September sun was still high in the sky. Salty perspiration was stinging Marco's eyes. After dropping his one piece of luggage in his room, Marco walked a short block away from the hotel, mindful of staying in the cooler shadows. He was skittish and decided it was best to stay off the main square on the slight chance that Paul just might come walking along. Instead, he decided to have a drink at a shaded café down a narrow side street. The shade was cool and welcoming. One drink led to another, and by the time he paid the waiter an hour later, he was slightly drunk.

When Marco returned to his hotel, he asked for a table in the courtyard and ordered a light meal. The waiter asked if he wanted to see the wine list. He thought better of it and declined. He was already pushing his limit, and he feared more alcohol might cause him to revisit the question of what he was doing there, raise doubt about the wisdom of the journey, and even question whether he would have been better off in some respects if he had never met Paul. He asked himself whether his overriding desire merely was to be free of the uncertainty that tormented him. He took that thought to bed with him.

*

When morning came, Marco decided this would be the day for his visit to Hotel Doña María. He supposed it was as close to Paul's Spain as he was likely to ever get. As he approached the hotel, Marco could not help but think about the recent pace of events. Two days earlier, he was in Buenos Aires. Now, he was in a massive square of ancient stones underfoot, standing at the base of the

Cathedral, *La Giralda*, one of the most important structures in this magnificent city. With the Cathedral on one side and the Real Alcazar on the other, he understood why this square was designated a world heritage site. It occurred to Marco that he had often dreamed of traveling to Spain, and there he finally was under these strange circumstances.

The hotel had been a former palace just steps from the Cathedral. It was a four-star establishment, which meant it was expensive. It occurred to Marco that this was an odd place for Paul to have come if he had fled Argentina. It was too visible and crowded with people from every continent. It was too conspicuous. Wouldn't a refugee—and that's what Marco would have been—seek to blend into society rather than to stand out? Marco also wondered who would have financed Paul's stay at this hotel, even temporarily. For the first time, Marco considered the possibility that there was a side of Paul he knew nothing about. Maybe he *was* a secret member of a band of leftist urban guerillas, possibly even the Montoneros, as some had asserted over the years.

*

Upon arrival at the Doña María, Marco decided it was best to stay away from the front entrance. He quickly ducked into the rear of the dark, ornate lobby, where he would be somewhat hidden from the coming and going guests but still be able to see them. He sat there immobile for the better part of the morning, mulling over his plan.

He would wait until the lobby was clear, then approach the registration desk and ask the clerk whether Paul was a past or current guest. It was just after noon by the time he approached the clerk. The clerk politely and apologetically informed him that he was not at liberty to divulge the information Marco was seeking.

It was almost three o'clock when Marco returned to his hotel. Despite the hazy sun and exhausting humidity, the square was still brimming with life. Marco planned to take a nap. Before going to his room, he reserved a table for dinner, hoping to have a quiet meal later that evening. However, as Marco passed through the lobby, the desk clerk called out to him, "Señor, there is a message for you."

Marco thought the clerk must have been mistaken. No one except his travel agent knew he was there. Then, a chilling possibility crossed his mind. It was possible that Paul was living in Seville after all, and he had spotted Marco in Doña María's lobby earlier in the day. Marco had not considered that his and Paul's meeting might be on Paul's terms. The attendant seemed to sense Marco's angst. "The Señor asked me to hand this to you personally and to tell you that he would like you to join him in the courtyard this evening."

The note was written on the hotel's stationery. The handwriting was immediately familiar to Marco. *I apologize for surprising you like this. May we meet in the courtyard at twenty-two hundred hours?* The note took Marco completely by surprise and stunned him like a bolt of lightning. It was signed, *Santiago.*

Marco could not imagine what Santiago was doing here, now, or how he found him. Then he remembered calling Santiago on the telephone the day after Lupi identified Santiago as the person who told him Paul had fled to Spain. Santiago confirmed what Lupi said. However, Santiago went on to explain that he initially heard it from their father and, further, that he had no firsthand knowledge about Paul's fate. That said, he asked Marco what it would take for him to finally put his memories of Paul behind him. Marco then told Santiago, as he later told Long, that he had yet to settle some things concerning Paul in his own mind. In response to Santiago asking what 'things' he was talking about, Marco revealed how he came upon the strange file in their father's library and later found that it contained a handwritten note placing Paul in Seville. In response to Santiago's further questioning, Marco told him that, *yes*, he planned to travel to Seville as soon as the Commission wrapped up its work.

When his mind re-focused on the present, Marco entertained the possibility that Santiago might have followed him to Seville to lend his support. But he quickly dismissed that thought as unlikely—the brothers had not been close since they were young. Marco could not think of any good reason for Santiago's presence; he had never been sympathetic to what he considered to be Marco's fixation on Paul's fate. Marco pondered the possibility that Santiago was the one who planted the idea in the father's mind that Paul was queer. He became annoyed and resentful. The likelihood of Santiago doing any good here seemed remote.

*

Marco's attempted afternoon siesta was fitful. Sleep was impossible. He got out of bed and dressed, filled with curiosity and unease. Again, he questioned the fragile confidence he had been feeling just a few days before.

Santiago was already seated when Marco arrived in the courtyard. He tried not to display his nerves when Santiago waved him to his table. Santiago rose but did not lean in for a traditional exchange of light kisses on the cheeks. Rather, Marco sat down and offered an obligatory hello and then just stated the obvious; he was surprised to see Santiago in Seville and wondered why he was there. Santiago passed over the implied question. Instead, he embarked, also nervously, on banal small talk focused mostly on pointless remarks about the weather and how hot and humid it still was.

The waiter came to take their drink order. Just after the waiter left for the bar, Santiago suddenly and pointedly asked Marco the reason he was in Seville. Naturally, Marco expected the question to be asked, but Santiago's timing took him by surprise. Further, he was startled by Santiago's tone of voice. There was nothing gladsome about it. Rather, it was straightforward and serious. After a few moments, during which Santiago stared into his eyes, Marco replied, "Perhaps it might be more appropriate for me to ask you the same question."

Another pause ensued. Then Santiago asked bluntly, "Please tell me why you are here." Marco lowered his voice slightly. "Your question strikes me as ironic and hardly coincidental. *You* apparently followed me here, and now you are asking *me* for an explanation?" Marco scoffed. The tension now between them seemed to be up to Marco to relieve. Marco understood this on a visceral level. He knew he probably owed Santiago an explanation for how he was behaving. *Indeed,* Marco thought, *he probably owed his entire family an explanation for the way he had been acting since Paul's disappearance eight years ago.* He wondered if it was just his nature to be self-contained or whether his behavior really was strange. At that moment, Marco thought about his late father. Perhaps he had owed an explanation to him as well. But Marco was not ready to go there. He was afraid that once he and Santiago started speaking the truth, neither of them would know when to stop.

This time, Santiago broke the silence. "Was growing up in San Isidro so difficult for you?" he asked, with just a hint of accusation.

"For now, let's just say that Father was very domineering," Marco replied. "You must agree that we were never encouraged to speak or even think for ourselves." He added that he understood it was important in those days to keep one's thoughts to oneself and that Father was just trying to protect us, perhaps from Paul's fate. "I understand that, but…"

Santiago apparently did not want to discuss Marco's perceptions of their father's shortcomings. "Let's agree that's a topic for another time. I didn't come here to get into that."

Marco felt his heartbeat quickening. He realized at that moment that, for once in a very long time, he and Santiago were about to speak the truth. Strangely, it was at that very moment that Santiago all but demanded that Marco tell him why he was in Seville.

"If you really must know, and it is none of your business, I am looking for Paul. But I'm sure you have surmised that because here you are. I have to find out for sure whether Paul fled Argentina and is living near Seville. Your turn, brother."

"How do you know that?" Santiago asked. "Do you have any proof that he is here now?"

"I don't know if he actually is here in Seville, but I believe he may be in Spain."

"And you have come to be with him?" Santiago pushed harder.

"I am not sure. I thought so when I left Buenos Aires, but now I am not certain. I think it will be enough for me just to find out what happened to him."

"I get it," said Santiago.

"You *get* it? I don't think you do. I don't know how you could. You don't *get* me at all. Perhaps you never did." Marco volleyed back. "You just want to know if Paul and I were 'lovers,' by which it seems you mean sexually." Both brothers sat silently for what seemed like minutes.

"Funny, I can see it now. All of you are wondering what Paul and I were up to. Well, for what it's worth, you were then, and still are, missing the point. Paul was a good friend—perhaps the best friend I ever had. He represented something different than the other kids we grew up with. I loved Paul's mind. He used it to think independently. He got that from his mother. That's what really concerned Father. He viewed Paul as a subversive and, even worse, a subversive who dangerously had my ear." Then, his voice out of control, Marco stopped abruptly.

Santiago waited for Marco to break the silence. He knew it was best not to speak when others were deep in thought because the next thing said often was unexpected. Sure enough, Marco finally spoke. It was his turn to look Santiago straight in the eyes. He spoke slowly but steadily, eventually stating what had been bottled up inside him for years: "Paul and I *were* 'involved,' as you put it."

Santiago did not react right away. After pausing to ponder whether he had just heard what he thought he had, Santiago chose an upbeat and slightly superficial tone. "I am sure whatever you are referring to was no more than youthful indiscretion—likely an experiment of sorts. Lots of boys experience that kind of thing."

Marco's throat tightened. He just shook his head in disagreement and repeated the message more explicitly, "This may be what you came to Spain to hear. Yes, we were lovers... of sorts."

Now, Santiago was at a loss for words. Marco could not tell what he was thinking from the look on his face. Hoping to fill the awkward void, Marco defaulted to pragmatism and asked Santiago how long he planned to stay in Seville now that he had uncovered what he came for. But Santiago ignored the question. He was determined to go on. At that moment, Marco already regretted having said what he had. He wished he had never started down this path but understood that Santiago was correct. He had to finish now.

"Are you here because you want to pick up where you left off?"

"For Christ's sake, Santiago," Marco replied. "It has been years."

"But here you are. You have never forgotten him," Santiago said in a voice slightly less imperious.

"And that's why you think I am searching for Paul now?" Marco asked. "Perhaps to *pick up* where we left off?" Marco turned away, breathing fast and perspiring heavily. He could feel his emotions building.

Sensing Marco's rising anxiety, Santiago asked if he was all right.

"Yes," he replied while wiping his brow with a napkin. He did not understand what had come over him. "I am now realizing that I, too, was/am a victim of the Process. Granted, I was not swept up in it, but I now see how close I came."

When he started speaking again, Marco's voice was sharp and clipped but back under control. "This cannot be the full reason you followed me here. Why are *you* here? Why are you *really* here? Now it's your turn to explain."

Santiago thought they both had said enough that evening. He knew he was not prepared to say more. The answer to Marco's pointed question very likely would offend Marco, possibly irreparably, Santiago wanted time to gather his own thoughts. Santiago stated as much and asked Marco if he would be willing to resume the conversation in the morning. "In the meantime," Santiago said, "I will arrange an afternoon return to Washington." Then he excused himself.

*

The morning air was cool. When Santiago took his seat at the breakfast table, he seemed nervous and guarded. For his own part, Marco regretted having revealed the secret part of himself and wished his words could be retracted. He chalked it up to feeling like he did owe the family an explanation, not so much for being in Spain (he still felt that was none of their business), but for the way he had been behaving for most of his recent adult life. Some explanation was required for why he seemed ungrateful for what he had been given. It occurred to Marco that maybe he needed to explain it to himself as well.

Thinking there was no point in avoiding the obvious, Marco led off right to the point. "I am afraid I shocked you last evening." He explained that he had not intended to. Rather, he added, "I figured you and the family already had drawn your own conclusions, so there was no point in pretending any longer. You were pressing. Now you have it."

Marco asked if he was right and if his suspicions were correct.

"Yes," Santiago sighed.

"So, Father 'knew' about Paul and me?"

"He did. So did the headmaster at *Nacionale*. He suspected it and had you and Paul followed. *He* was the one who informed Father."

After another stretch of silence, Santiago went right back to the core question. "So, I gather you did come all this way to be, we'll say, *with* Paul again?"

"To *see* Paul? To find Paul. That was my plan," Marco replied. Marco explained how he initially wanted to see and be near Paul, and that seemed like a good idea when he boarded his flight in Buenos Aires. "But now, I am thinking it may not be such a wise idea," he confided. "My overriding desire has changed. Now, I just want to free myself from all the questions. I just want to know what happened."

"Father apparently made an effort to locate Paul," Marco explained. "There was a fat file among his personal papers that contained a lot of handwritten notes. Based on the handwriting, it must have been given to Father by someone else—perhaps the headmaster. Anyway, it had some sketchy information on Paul's whereabouts. One of many notes implied that Paul fled Argentina and was traced to here to Seville."

When he started speaking again, Marco was clipped. "So now you know *my* reason for coming. You have yet to state *yours*? I deserve an explanation from you."

The palpable tension between the brothers had risen again. Marco could see and feel it. Santiago's whole demeanor changed. His face bore an expression that Marco could not understand. It was like he had become a stranger. It was as if he was distant, no longer his older brother. But Marco sensed it was more than that.

"That's fair enough," Santiago eventually replied. "You've done the difficult job of clearing things up for me. I owe you the same consideration." Santiago asked for a few minutes to think. "What I have to say to you now can never be taken back. I need to find the right words."

Santiago began by stating that even before their father learned about the so-called 'indiscretion', he believed Paul was too open with his political leanings and his feelings about the military government.

Santiago asked, "Do you remember the night Paul came to one of Father's garden parties?" When Marco questioned what that had to do with anything, Santiago became more specific and asked whether he remembered meeting one of Father's colleagues, Señor Nestor Benitez. Marco did not. Santiago explained that he, Marco, apparently had introduced Paul to Sr. Benitez. Benitez drew Paul into a conversation during which Paul freely expressed his views on certain issues. "Among other things," Santiago went on, "they apparently talked about the plight of Argentina's poor. As I later heard it from Father, Paul felt strongly that the poor should not be blamed for their impoverishment and, shall we say, *strongly* made his point."

Santiago went on to explain that Benitez later recounted the conversation to their father, not without his own bias; he imagined and suggested to Father that such views and conversation could endanger not only Paul but also Marco and, by extension, the family. "As you know, Father was greatly concerned about that kind of scandal or threat of danger—anything that would damage your future or the family's reputation. I imagine he decided then that he had to separate you and Paul." Santiago had spouted the words as quickly as he could, possibly fearing that if he slowed or paused, they would not come out at all.

Santiago's expression changed as he waited for that thought to sink in. When he spoke again, he slowly explained. "You are right. The file you found was put together by your headmaster. Father borrowed it and, for some unknown reason, never returned it."

Before going on, Santiago swallowed and paused to collect himself. "Father told me about the file the last time I visited him. He gave it to me. I took it." Santiago paused for what seemed like minutes. "On the morning of Father's funeral, *I* put it in a place where I knew you eventually would find it." Then Santiago confessed that the note that purported to place Paul in Seville was fake, and he, Santiago, put it in the file. He had written it before the funeral after Marco had confronted him about Paul. Marco sat blank and silent.

"Why would you do that!" Marco demanded as he sat up and began to rise.

"I thought it would put you off the trail of the truth," Santiago explained how he hoped to bring Marco a measure of closure. Eventually, he added that he supposed he also wanted to protect their father. "I thought if you believed Paul had fled to Spain, you would change your assessment of him and stop what we all believed to be a dangerous and foolish quest. I never thought that it would come to this—that you would come here looking for him. Because Marco..." Santiago's voice trailed off. "Because Marco... the truth is... Paul is not here. Paul is dead."

Marco sank back into his chair, head reeling.

"Father had Paul arrested," Santiago said. "You must see that giving up Paul to the Process was Father's way of keeping you and the family out of everything that was happening, out of the chaos, the nightmare. It was his need to control and his duty to protect—as he saw it. I am very sorry to say that we later learned Paul had been taken to the ESMA and eventually 'transferred to the east'. Father told me 'transferred to the east' was military-speak for 'disappeared.'"

Buenos Aires
1978

At midnight on a cool Wednesday night in September, an Electra belonging to the Navy was being prepared for flight on the tarmac of the Santiago Newberry Military Airport. It had been a damp and dreary day with pewter gray skies. Inside an adjacent hangar, reluctant pilots and crew were sitting in a tight circle, tensely waiting for the military trucks delivering those they would be carrying. Earlier that day, the officers at Dorado, the command center where such orders originated, busily prepared the list of prisoners that were slated to 'fly'. As soon as night fell, guards took to the corridors of the ESMA and gathered the unfortunate ones.

Paul Casales was number thirty on that day's list.

Assembled in the basement of the officers' mess, Paul was told he was being transferred to a working farm in the north where there would be no more beatings, and he would be prepared for his eventual release. He was also told that before being loaded into a truck for transport to the airport, Paul would have to be vaccinated against certain diseases that were prevalent in the north. That was a lie. In fact, he was given a shot of Pen-Naval, a powerful tranquilizer intended to immobilize him and eventually render him close to unconscious.

When the truck arrived at the airport, it passed through a gate in the chain link fencing and, lights out, drove onto the tarmac and up to the idling Electra. It took two soldiers to lift Paul into the cargo hold in the back of the airplane. One had his hands, and the other took his feet. Eventually, a total of thirty prisoners were lifted into the same hold. All, including Paul, were virtually paralyzed but vaguely conscious.

The pilots had been selected randomly. Their mission was supposed to be secret, but as soon as they received the flight plan (*Fly directly to Punta Indio, where you will be contacted for additional instructions*), they knew from rumors that they were piloting a 'death flight'.

Wheels up.

As they approached Punta Indio, the pilots were ordered to jam the aircraft's navigational systems and continue out over the Atlantic Ocean, radio silent, on a due easterly heading.

Then came morning. As soon as the first light appeared on the horizon, the radio crackled to life. The pilots received instructions to give the order to open the Electra's rear hatch and, upon completion of their mission, to silently return to Buenos Aires.

The crew worked in teams of two. They lifted each prisoner by their arms and legs and dragged them toward the open hatch. Dutifully and silently, they heaved their barely conscious quarry into the howling thin air.

Fish food.

Printed in the USA
CPSIA information can be obtained
at www.ICGtesting.com
LVHW091117221024
794498LV00007B/394